THE SADDLE BUM

PHILIP KETCHUM

SAGEBRUSH
Large Print Westerns

First published in Great Britain by Consul
First published in the United States by Popular Library

First Isis Edition
published 2018
by arrangement with
Golden West Literary Agency

A catalogue record for this book is available
from the British Library.

ISBN 978–1–78541–561–6 (pb)

Published by
F. A. Thorpe (Publishing)
Anstey, Leicestershire

Set by Words & Graphics Ltd.
Anstey, Leicestershire
Printed and bound in Great Britain by
T. J. International Ltd., Padstow, Cornwall

This book is printed on acid-free paper

THE SADDLE BUM

After plummeting cattle prices lost Gil Daly his ranch, he drifted for a year, resentful at being branded a saddle bum. Now he works for the Swallowfork — but after only a week there, he already dislikes it and is planning to move on. When his fellow ranch hands assault and hang a suspected rustler, despite the man's protestations of innocence, Gil decides he's finished with the Swallowfork. But the Swallowfork isn't finished with him. Colin Brewster, son of the owner, roughs him up and leaves him bleeding. So, despite being offered work at two other ranches, Gil turns the jobs down in favour of sniffing around and finding out what's really going on. For he has a score to settle with the Brewsters — and he suspects there was more to that hanging than hot-headed cowboys angry over lost cattle . . .

CHAPTER ONE

Brewster routed them out before dawn. The cook had breakfast ready. They ate in a hurry, then saddled up and headed south, Lou Crowell leading the way. There wasn't much talk. There hadn't been much talk at breakfast. Once, Dan Brewster, who owned the Swallowfork, looked over at one of his men and said, "Frank, you head for Antioch and get the sheriff." But immediately he changed his mind: "No. Let it go. We'll handle this ourselves. We don't need the sheriff to deal with a man caught rustling."

Gil Daly rode with Tom Ash, eating a share of the dust kicked up by the six riders ahead. He didn't know Ash very well. For that matter, he didn't feel he knew any of the men on the Swallowfork, except by name. He hadn't been here long. Only a week. He wouldn't be here much longer. He didn't like Swallowfork or the man who owned it or the men who worked here. There wasn't much point in staying where you didn't feel comfortable, where you weren't accepted, where you didn't belong.

The sun was up by the time they made it to the south fork of the Rhymer River. There they stopped for a few minutes, to water and rest their horses and have a smoke. And there, Lou Crowell gave them a brief story of what had happened the night before. Crowell was tall, gaunt, stoop-shouldered, about forty. Gil hadn't seen him before this morning. With a man referred to only as Hondo, Crowell had been combing the hilly country south and west of here for strays.

"We rounded up about forty head from the pockets in the hills," Crowell said, "and shagged them down into the basin. That was a couple days ago. Then we turned back, working farther south, and picked up a few more head. After we shagged them down we noticed where a batch of cattle had been driven south toward Squaw Creek. We couldn't figure why anyone had been driving Swallowfork cattle south, so we followed the trail, guessing maybe someone had picked up the first batch we had shagged down from the hills. Rustlers, I mean."

"Sidwell or Logan," Brewster said heavily. "They've both been fattening themselves on Swallowfork cattle."

Max Sidwell and Howard Logan, Gil had learned, were two ranchers whose land bordered on the Swallowfork below Squaw Creek.

"Anyhow," Crowell said, "about fifteen miles from here we sighted this man riding a lame horse. When he saw us coming he started to run, even though his horse was in pretty bad shape. That was a dead giveaway that he was one of the rustlers, trailing behind on account of his horse. We took him without much of a fight. Hondo's got him at the Squaw Creek line shack."

"A good day's work, Lou," said Dan Brewster. "What's the fellow's name?"

"He says his name's Ed Farley. And he says he's not a rustler."

There was a general laugh at that. Someone said, "No rustler ever admitted it, not even with a rope around his neck."

"But this man will," Brewster said. "He'll admit it and he will tell us who he's working for."

Brewster was big, thick-bodied, heavy. His ruddy features were half hidden by a mustache and beard and the hat pulled low on his forehead. Under the hat he was bald. He had black eyes. Steady eyes. Hard eyes. The look in them could hit at a man almost with the force of a blow. Sitting on a horse to his left was his son, Colin, a man of twenty-six or twenty-seven — Gil's age. Colin, short and heavy, with powerful shoulders, was built much like his father, and perhaps was like his father. Gil couldn't be sure. In the older man's presence, Colin always hung back, seldom having anything to say. When his father wasn't around, though, Colin became an imitation of what Dan Brewster might be if he ever cut loose. Colin had a quick and ugly temper, and he showed it.

Gil glanced at the others in the group, at the men who were little more than names to him: Hank Morse and Slim Gorman, Tom Ash and Frank Mills. The expressions they wore matched the look on Brewster's face, and perhaps there was reason for it, reason he couldn't feel. They were Swallowfork. This rustling was something they had lived with, something they would be glad to pin down. If he had been here longer he might feel as they did, but he was an outsider, a man who didn't belong.

Brewster wheeled toward the south. "Let's ride," he said. "Let's get there and get it over with."

They moved on again, Gil once more falling in with Tom Ash and wondering, uneasily, why he had come along. But there was a blunt answer to that. He had taken a job with Brewster, and when a man took a job he did what the job required, whether it was mending fences, hunting strays or riding after rustlers. If a man didn't like it, he quit, but until he quit he stuck with the others.

It was a rugged country they were traveling through now. The hills were wooded with scrub pine and oak. Gil hadn't been on this part of the range but he could see at once how two men could be kept busy all year, just combing out strays. It occurred to him to wonder why the Swallowfork didn't fence off this entire area. Certainly it was more of a liability than an asset.

The Squaw Creek line shack nestled in a narrow valley through which a creek twisted its irregular way to the basin. It was set back in a high grove of trees, almost hidden from sight. The man called Hondo waited at the door in front of it. He was an oldish man with a deeply wrinkled face and watery, pale blue eyes. Gray whiskers bristled on his chin.

"Where's the rustler?" Brewster asked as they reined up.

"Inside," Hondo said. "Shall I bring him out?"

The Swallowfork owner nodded. "Yeah, bring him out. Where's the horse he was riding?"

4

"Tied over there near mine. The gray."

"Go see the brand on it, Colin," said Brewster.

Colin swung to the ground. He moved to where the two horses were tied, studied the gray for a moment, then came back. "Circle H brand," he reported. "Never heard of it before but that doesn't mean anything."

The older man shrugged his shoulders. He was staring at the open door to the line shack. Gil looked that way, too. He heard the sound of a ruckus inside, heard Hondo swearing, saw a man appear in the doorway. The man seemed to lean there momentarily. Then, as Hondo thrust at his shoulders, the man came pitching forward, lost his balance, and fell. A whining cry broke from his lips as he went down, and he didn't get up. Quite possibly, he couldn't. His wrists were tied together at his back.

Most of the Swallowfork riders had dismounted and now Gil Daly swung to the ground. He was slender, not noticeably tall. He had a thin, sun-tanned face, hair almost the color of straw, and gray eyes which looked troubled. He trailed the reins of his horse, then moved toward the others who had gathered around the rustler. There was a distinct reluctance in his walk, and he kept scowling.

The rustler, if he was a rustler, had been pulled to his feet. A Swallowfork rider stood on each side of him, holding him erect. He looked about fifty, or he might have been older. What little hair he had was stringy, gray, and long. He needed a shave. His clothing was old and dirty; it probably hadn't been changed in weeks.

5

There was fear in his eyes and in his quick, deep breathing. Perspiration showed on his forehead.

Dan Brewster stood in front of him, slightly hunched forward, both fists clenched. Brewster's voice bellowed at him.

"Who hired you? Who sent you after my cattle?"

The man shook his head. "I wasn't after your cattle. I was on my way to Antioch."

"You weren't riding that way when you were caught."

"My horse had gone lame. I was cutting toward Sidwell's."

"So you know Sidwell. You were working for Sidwell."

"But I wasn't. I was —"

Brewster's fist whipped up. It caught the man squarely in the face, jolting him backward. He would have fallen, save for the two men who were holding him up.

"You're lying," Brewster said. "Who were you working for — Sidwell or Logan?"

Blood had spurted from the man's nose and was now running over his mouth and chin and dripping down on his dirty shirt. His body sagged between the two Swallowfork riders.

"You'd better talk, and talk fast," Brewster said. "Someone bring me a rope."

"Here you are," Frank Mills said quietly.

Gil glanced sideways at Frank Mills, who had been standing there with the rope ready. Mills was short and fat and had a funny little figure. But he was quick for a fat man, and constantly active. He was foreman of

Swallowfork, but didn't have many of the responsibilities of a foreman. His puffy face was moist with perspiration. Gil mopped his own forehead. He was perspiring, too, though the sun wasn't yet hot.

Brewster took the rope, then handed it back. "Put it around his neck," he ordered. "Colin, get his horse. We'll move over there to the trees."

Colin led up the gray, which was limping quite badly. Frank Mills fastened the rope around the man's neck, drew the noose tight, and stepped back, holding the coiled slack.

"You ready to talk?" Brewster asked. "You ready to talk, or shall we go ahead?"

The man stiffened a little. His head turned from side to side as he looked at the men who stood around him. His lips moved. "I was prospecting in the Toltecs with Pete Enders. I was on my way to Antioch with some ore samples. I don't know anything about the rustling. Honest to God, I don't. Gimme a chance. You've got to gimme a chance. You've gotta —"

Brewster stepped forward. Again his fist slashed into the man's face, and again the man on each side of the rustler held him up.

"I want the truth!" Brewster roared. "I want it now! Who were you working for?"

Brewster's face was flushed, ugly. His fists were still clenched. Gil had the sudden feeling that nothing the rustler might say would save him, because Brewster was in no condition to recognize the truth if it didn't match what he wanted to hear. Rage had driven the man out of control.

"Who was it," Brewster shouted again. "Logan or Sidwell?"

But the rustler was in no shape to make any reply. His head sagged forward on his breast. He was a dead weight to the men who were holding him.

"Put him on his horse," Brewster said, jerking away. "Bring him over to the trees."

Gil pulled off his hat. He ran his fingers through his hair. He swallowed a couple of times. His stomach was churning. A voice in his mind was telling him that any man ought to have more of a chance than this, a chance to prove his words, to test his story.

"Well, what's the matter with you?" asked a sudden voice in front of him. "Don't you like it?"

Gil looked up. He stiffened. Dan Brewster had stopped and was facing him, a crooked, ugly grin on his face. Brewster was bending slightly forward, hunched toward him just as he had hunched toward the rustler. That hard, direct stare was a violent challenge.

"Well?" Brewster snapped.

Gil took a deep breath. He moistened his lips. A sudden, rebellious recklessness swept over him. He heard a voice which must have been his own, a voice saying, "What if I don't?"

"Then you don't belong on Swallowfork," Brewster said.

"So I don't belong on Swallowfork," Gil said.

The others, moving toward the trees, had stopped and were looking back at them. Then, as though some magic had abruptly cleared the muddy waters of his thinking, Gil saw the picture of what was happening here with a startling clarity. A crowd of Swallowfork riders had caught a man who they thought was a rustler. They were dealing with him according to their own pattern. With them was a new hand, untried and untested, a man of unknown qualities. He would fit in with them now, or be thrown out.

Brewster was shaking his head. "No, you don't belong on Swallowfork. You'll draw your time today, when we hit town."

"I'll take it now, if you want me to," said Gil.

"You'll take it when we get to town. Anything else you've got to say?"

He was out of it. He didn't have to say anything else. But the words were there in his throat and they came out.

"Yes, one thing more. The man you're going to lynch might not be a rustler. His story might be true."

Anger flamed in Brewster's face. "He's a rustler, and I'll prove it. You'll hear it from his own lips. And after we've taken care of him, we'll take care of you."

Gil stood motionless. He didn't quite know what Brewster meant by that. He was wearing his gun. He could whip it up pretty quickly. But if it came to that, he didn't have only Brewster to consider. Every man here would be against him. He glanced at Colin who stood silent and watchful near his father, at Tom Ash and Slim Gorman just beyond them, at the two mounted men on each side of the rustler, and at the chunky figure of Frank Mills who still carried the coiled rope. Bleak stares probed back at him, as though at a stranger, as though at someone they'd never seen before. The week he had spent on Swallowfork didn't count.

"Come along," Brewster said.

Under the trees, they stopped. Mills threw the rope over a branch above the rustler's head, pulled it tight enough to straighten the man's body, then fastened it around the trunk of the tree and stepped forward to hold the horse steady. The two men who had ridden here with the rustler, dismounted. Brewster moved around so he could look up into the rustler's face.

"Farley?" he called. "Did you say your name was Farley?"

"That's right," the rustler said in a husky whisper. "But I was prospecting in the Toltecs with Pete —"

"You were not prospecting in the Toltecs," Brewster shouted. "I want the truth. I want the name of the man who hired you to run off Swallowfork cattle. Was it Sidwell or Logan?"

The rustler gulped. He licked the blood from his lips. He looked down at Brewster, his eyes wide, distended by fear. He was sucking in deep gulps of air as though in an effort to store it up against the time when the rope around his neck would choke off his supply.

"Your last chance, Farley," Brewster called. "Which man was it? Sidwell or Logan?"

"If I tell you," said the rustler, still in a husky whisper. "If I tell you —"

"Anything you want, Farley," Brewster agreed, and there was a triumphant lift in his voice. "Just give me the name."

"It was — Logan."

10

"Logan, huh," Brewster murmured. "Logan! I knew it." He rubbed his hands together. "Logan. Howard Logan."

"And now this rope," the rustler quavered. "You promised —"

Brewster looked at Frank Mills and nodded. Mills stepped away suddenly, slapping the gray horse on the shoulder. The horse danced sideways, pulling Farley against the rope. A high, shrill cry broke from the rustler's lips. He struggled with his legs to pull the horse back but his jerking and twisting body only excited the horse to jump forward. The rope around the rustler's throat tightened, bringing a whistling end to his cry. It dragged him from the saddle and left him twisting and jerking at it's end.

Gil had moved forward involuntarily. He was shocked at the suddenness of what had happened. He heard Mills saying, "Well, what do you know about that. I just let go the reins for a minute to scratch myself. I reckon Farley must have jabbed the horse with his heels."

Someone laughed. Gil's eyes flicked that way. Colin was watching the twisting figure at the end of the rope as though in the grip of a horrible fascination. His mouth hung open. His breath was coming fast. There were two quick shots from Gil's left. The body at the ends of the rope relaxed, then started twisting slowly around and around, a spreading, dark stain showing below the throat.

Tom Ash had fired the shots. He put his gun away, glanced quickly at Brewster, mopped a hand over his face, and muttered something under his breath.

"So it was Logan," said Brewster. "Howard Logan. You all heard what the rustler said. We'll face Logan with this and see which way he crawls."

No one offered any comment. No one, Gil noticed, was staring any longer at the rustler's body. Two men had gone after the gray. Frank Mills was checking his gun. Hondo was rolling a cigaret, but having trouble with it. Colin was staring at his father, an almost violent look in his eyes.

Brewster pulled off his hat and smoothed his hand over his bald head. He said, "Mills, cut the rustler's body down. We'll tie him on Hondo's horse and take him in to town with us so the sheriff won't have to come out here. Crowell can ride to the ranch and get Hondo a fresh horse."

Frank Mills nodded.

"And now, you," Brewster growled, facing Gil Daly. "What have you got to say?"

Gil had been expecting this. He had loosened the gun in his holster though he wasn't sure a gun would be of much help. An answer formulated itself in his mind. He could tell Brewster the rustler's confession was not forced, and that what he had admitted was unproven. But there was really no point in saying anything. Nothing would be gained by further antagonizing these men.

"So you don't have anything to say? Is that it?" asked Brewster.

Gil shrugged.

"You heard his confession, didn't you?"

"I heard it," said Gil.

12

"Didn't I tell you, you would?"

Again Gil shrugged. He watched Brewster closely. And Brewster was watching him, a faintly puzzled look in his eyes, as though not quite sure about him, or sure of what he should do. Or as though trying to measure him against some set of standards. Finally he succeeded in matching things up.

"Just a saddle bum," he said. "A saddle bum. We should never have taken you on. You'll ride with us to Antioch and draw your pay. If you're smart, you won't even go back to Swallowfork for your stuff —" he spat deliberately — "saddle bum."

CHAPTER
TWO

Gil Daly moved back to where his horse was standing. He checked the cinch strap, which didn't need checking. He combed his fingers through the horse's mane. He said words under his breath, profane words which had no meaning and which brought him little relief. Suddenly he felt shaky. The backs of his knees were aching. He dug into his pocket for tobacco and started making a cigaret but the first paper tore. He tried it again more carefully. "I've seen things like this before," he told himself. "Why did it have to get me?"

But he hadn't. Not exactly like this. Not so crude.

He lit his cigaret and watched what was happening. Frank Mills lowered the rustler's body to the ground and loosened the rope from around his neck. Now he was recoiling it. Hondo had gone to the line shack and was bringing back a blanket. Two men, Gorman and Crowell, were hunkered over the rustler's body and seemed to be going through his pockets. What they found they were piling on a neckerchief.

"A little money, a couple of letters, some tobacco, the usual stuff," Crowell said. "What do we do with it, Brewster?"

"Tie it up and put it in one of my saddlebags," Brewster ordered. "I'll turn it over to the sheriff."

Brewster was standing on one side, talking to Frank Mills.

Hank Morse, one of the men who had gone after the rustler's horse, approached Brewster. He was carrying a canvas sack about twice the size of a money-bag. It was bulky.

"What about this stuff?" he asked.

"What is it?" Brewster asked.

"It might be the ore samples the rustler said he had. I found it in one of the saddlebags on the gray."

Brewster took the sack, opened it, and looked inside. "If these are ore samples, I'll eat them," he declared. "But just to prove it we'll take them along and show them to Kemp at the assay office. Stuff them in my saddlebag."

Gil Daly pinched out his cigaret. He walked to the creek for a drink of water. There, almost hidden by a screen of shrubbery at the creek's edge, Colin Brewster was leaning over, heaving. Horrible sounds came from his throat. Then he heard Gil's step. He straightened and stared at Gil, his eyes blazing.

Gil got down on his knees. He cupped up water in his hands and drank it. He heard Colin start away, then stop and turn back. He knew Colin was standing above him, and he knew how Colin felt. No man liked being caught in a moment of weakness.

"The quicker you get out of this country, the better it'll be for you, Daly."

15

Gil took another drink which he didn't want. He heard Colin move away. After a moment he stood up and walked to his horse. Colin Brewster, not far away, was still staring at him. Quite deliberately, Colin drew his gun, checked it, then shoved it back into its holster. There was an implied threat in the gesture.

The rustler's body, wrapped in a blanket, had been tied on Hondo's horse. Mills held the lead rope. Brewster and the others were mounting.

"You ride with me, Ash," said Brewster.

He gave no reason for this and it seemed to Gil that Tom Ash looked surprised. But Ash made no comment. He was a man of about fifty, thin and stooped and usually silent. He had a reddish face, the kind of skin that wouldn't tan and was always raw and sore from the sun and wind.

No other proscribed orders were given for their ride to Antioch, but as they started away, Frank Mills fell in beside Gil. "Let's stick close behind Brewster and Ash," Mills said. "That way, we won't get so much dust."

That way, also, most of the Swallowfork riders were behind Gil Daly. But perhaps there was no meaning in it.

It was a long, and hot, and tiring ride to Antioch — a cross country ride with hills to climb and descend and with no road to follow until they were almost there. It was a ride in the heat of the day, and in the late summer this was a hot country. There was no breath of wind. By night, there would be. The nights were cool. The nights were always something to look forward to.

16

To Gil, this was particularly true of the night just ahead. He would be paid off at Antioch. He would be on his own again, without much money, but a free agent. Free to go where he wanted. A saddle bum? He shook his head. He wasn't a saddle bum, exactly. He could stick with a job, and had. Up to a year ago, he had been as steady as they come. He had started working for wages at sixteen. He had saved his money. At twenty-four he had owned his own brand. At twenty-six he had been sold out, losing everything. There was some satisfaction, but not much, in realizing that skidding cattle prices and tightening credits had been largely responsible for his failure, and that not he alone but many men had gone under a year ago. There was some satisfaction in an awareness of what he had learned as a ranch owner. Some, but not much. And starting over again wasn't easy. In fact, he hadn't started. For a year he had drifted . . . but a year of drifting didn't make him a saddle bum.

In the late afternoon, Antioch appeared suddenly just ahead of them, and as he stared toward it, Gil realized that he was hungry. Quite hungry. But so were the rest of these men. In starting out they hadn't anticipated the necessity of a ride to town, hence had brought no food.

"Nice town, Antioch," Frank Mills said abruptly.

He hadn't talked much on the way in, and now he was talking mainly to himself, for he didn't glance at Gil as he spoke. And Gil made no answer. He didn't know how nice a town Antioch was. He had spent only a few hours there. He had ridden in, had asked about a job, had been directed to Brewster who was in town that day, and had been hired. At dusk he had ridden with Brewster to Swallowfork. His vague memory of the town recalled a main street with several stores, several saloons, a bank, a hotel, and a corral. Back of the main street on each side were clustering houses. The Rhymer River, a stream without much water in it, made a bend around the west side of the town. It was the same Rhymer River which cut through the basin of the Swallowfork.

"Yep," said Frank Mills. "A good town, Antioch. And you can get a good steak at the Antioch House."

A brief smile touched Gil's lips. It was like Frank Mills to think of food. The fat, chunky foreman of the Swallowfork had always been the first man at the table at the ranch, and the last to leave it. Others here might be thinking of a drink, but with Frank Mills, food was more important. And more important, probably, than a report to the sheriff on the death of the man whose body was on the horse Mills was leading.

After they had crossed the bridge over the Rhymer River and reached the outskirts of the town, Brewster pulled up. The others gathered around him.

"We'll leave our horses at the corral," said Brewster. "Tom Ash will stay there with the rustler's body. I'll see the sheriff. The rest of you will walk on to the Teton Saloon and stay there until I show up. I don't want any talk about what happened. If Logan's in town I want to spring this on him myself."

No one offered any objections.

18

Brewster looked at Gil Daly. "I'll see you at the Teton. I'll have your money."

Gil shrugged his shoulders. He had ten dollars coming. Ten dollars for a week's work. He wondered if Brewster didn't have that much money in his pocket right now, and why the man didn't just pay him and have it over.

They rode on. Near the first houses two dogs came barking into the road, and in the back yard of one of the houses, a woman in a long shapeless and colorless dress, who was taking in the washing, stopped her work to stare at them. Ahead, up the main street of the town, Gil could see a scattering of horses at the tie-rails, and two teams and wagons. There were several men in sight.

Beyond the first few houses was Tarbow's Corral. They pulled up into the yard and dismounted near the watering trough. Ollie Tarbow came out, calling a greeting, and then looked quite sober as he saw the blanket-wrapped figure on the Mills' led-horse.

"Just don't ask any questions, Tarbow," said Brewster. "Ash is going to stay here for a while with the body we brought in."

"Sure, Dan. That's all right," Tarbow said quickly.

He moistened his lips. He was an awkward-looking man, tall, lanky, and with one shoulder lower than the other. His shirt sleeves were rolled up over skinny arms. He might have been thirty or fifty. It was hard to tell.

Gil led his horse to the watering trough and stood there a moment, feeling the stiffness from the ride. He pulled off his hat and ran his fingers through his hair. It was sticky, dirty, and needed a barbering. But he

19

wouldn't get it here. He would get it up north somewhere, or back to the south. There would be more riding for him tonight, as soon as he collected his ten dollars and after he had something to eat. North, he told himself, reaching a decision. And I'll stop at the Swallowfork and pick up my stuff, too.

He turned away, brushing past Tom Ash as he started toward the street.

"Make a break for it, Daly," Ash said, under his breath.

Gil Daly almost stopped. He caught his breath. He started to look around toward. Ash but saw Brewster watching him.

"Let's get going," Brewster said.

Gil continued on toward the street. Slim Gorman fell in beside him and Hank Morse came up on the other side. Brewster and Mills walked ahead. Colin Brewster trailed behind. They had him boxed, but perhaps that was accidental. It had to be accidental. If these men had meant to start anything, they had had a day-long opportunity better than this. Why had Ash warned him to make a break for it?

There was no logical answer.

Halfway up the main street, Dan Brewster cut across the street toward the sheriff's office. But he didn't at once go inside. Instead, he stopped on the porch of the building, pulled a cigar from his pocket, and lit it. Brewster didn't smoke much on the range. At night, when at Swallowfork, he limited himself to one cigar after dinner. But when in town he was smoking a cigar or chewing on one constantly. It was one of his props, though he never thought of it that way, never thought of it at all. The pattern had become habitual.

Looking back across the street, he watched his men moving in the direction of the Teton Saloon and nodded with satisfaction. He had a good crew, men who would stick by him, men whose minds were grooved in much the same fashion as his. Today's work had proved it. Only Ash had shown a soft spot. He had shot the rustler when the rope hadn't broken his neck. And he had shown his soft spot again in asking, on the way into town, what he meant to do about Gil Daly. Brewster hadn't answered the question. He had let Ash stew about it, knowing full well Ash expected the worst. Ash always did. He saw in every danger a calamity. Ash was weak. It was something to remember.

Brewster turned toward the door to the sheriff's office. Then, hearing the sound of horses on the street, he looked around. Coming in from the north, and now passing him, were Sam Chenoweth and his daughter, Myra. The Chenoweth ranch lay far to the north, bordering at one point on the Swallowfork. It wasn't large. Sam ran it with the help of one man, and his daughter. Part of the year he didn't even keep the man. Sam was a tall, grave man, who always looked worried. Myra, who was about twenty-five, had her father's slender figure. She was dark-haired, attractive. There had been a time when Brewster wondered about having Myra on the Swallowfork. His own wife had died five years before, and the only women now on the Swallowfork were Frank Mill's wife and the dumpy woman who helped her with the meals. Myra Chenoweth would

21

have graced the Swallowfork, but she wasn't interested. One night she had told him so. Brewster's face burned anew at the memory of her words. But he touched his hat to the Chenoweths as they passed. Sam returned the salute. Myra looked straight at him, then looked away with no sign of recognition.

Brewster was scowling and angry as he jerked open the door to the sheriff's office and stepped inside. He slammed the door shut. "Wake up," he roared at Carl Huggins. "Get your feet off the desk."

"It's my desk," Huggins said mildly. But he swung his feet to the floor, straightening in his chair and reaching for his pipe. He was a thin, bony man, with iron gray hair, and dark, deep set eyes. He always looked tired, and the first impression he gave was of an easy going nature. But there was a stubborn streak in his make up. Brewster had measured it on several occasions. An awareness of it entered his mind now.

"I've got a job for you," he said slowly.

Huggins tamped tobacco into his pipe. "Yeah? What kind of job?"

"We caught a man last night rustling Swallowfork cattle. His body's down at the corral."

"Dead?" said Huggins, frowning.

"Of course he's dead," Brewster said, an edge of irritation in his voice. "I said we caught him rustling, didn't I?"

"Who shot him?"

Brewster's teeth clamped down on his cigar. "What difference does that make? The important thing is, he was working for Howard Logan."

22

"How do you know he was?"

"He admitted it."

"And then you shot him?"

Brewster slammed both hands down on the desk and leaned half across it. "I said the man was a rustler, didn't I? What do you do with rustlers?"

"You arrest them, and they stand trial," Huggins said. "It there's any executing, it's done under the law."

Brewster straightened. "And so what?"

"I don't know," Huggins said, climbing to his feet. "I don't know, Brewster, but I don't like it. And there are others who won't like it."

"To hell with them."

"That won't solve anything."

"I still say, to hell with them."

Huggins reached for his hat and put it on.

"Where are you going?" Brewster asked.

"Down to the corral to see the body you brought in."

"And what about Logan."

"I'll talk to Logan."

"You'll talk to him? This calls for more than talk."

"There's already been more than talk. Where did it happen? The rustling?"

"On the south range of Swallowfork," Brewster said. "Just above Squaw Creek. Some forty or fifty head of cattle are missing."

"I'll probably be riding that way tomorrow," Huggins said, moving toward the door. "Do you have someone you can send with me?"

Dan Brewster sucked in a deep breath. He had half anticipated this attitude on the part of Carl Huggins.

There was no point in getting riled up about it. Huggins would move slowly and deliberately in whatever he did. But however slowly he moved, the main thing now was to get him started in the direction of Logan. He might not like the fact that the rustler they had caught had been killed, but he couldn't get too excited over a dead rustler. And even though the sheriff's sympathies might be with the small ranchers since he had once been one, he would have to stand behind the Swallowfork in cracking down on men like Logan.

"I've got two men working out of a line shack on Squaw Creek," said Brewster. "They can show you where the cattle were rustled."

"I know where the line shack is," Huggins said. He opened the door, stepped out on the porch, then looked back. "Leave Logan to me."

Dan Brewster moved to the door, went outside and closed it. He watched the lanky, ungainly figure of the sheriff walking down the street in the direction of the corral. He said under his breath, "All right. You can have Logan. What there is left of him after I finish. This part of the country needs a lesson."

He repeated those, last words again, nodding his head. Logan wasn't the only rancher around here who had been growing fat on Swallowfork cattle. There were others just as guilty. Swallowfork had taken it for too long. The time had come to call a halt.

He turned up the street in the direction of the Teton Saloon, a big, heavy, square-shouldered man, scowling in concentration on his thoughts and unaware of the

24

sticky heat of the late afternoon. He nodded to several men he passed but didn't stop to talk to them. He did, however, drop into the Emporium for a word with Ollie Schmidt.

"Has Logan been in today?" he asked the storekeeper.

"I haven't seen him," Schmidt said.

Brewster continued on toward the Teton. If Logan had come to town today he would have stopped at the Emporium. He always did. Since Schmidt hadn't seen him, it was a good bet he wasn't here. That meant that if he wanted to see Logan, he would have to ride to Logan's place, which might be a good idea, anyhow.

But first, there was the problem of Gil Daly. Not a problem, really. More of an annoyance. The saddle bum would cause them no trouble. He could be paid off and a couple of his men could see him well started on his way out of the valley. Brewster chuckled, recalling the fears of Tom Ash. There had been no point in making Gil Daly come to town with them. It had just worked out that way. He had said he would pay Daly when they got to town, and had stubbornly stuck to it.

The Teton Saloon was just ahead. A drink was just ahead. Dan Brewster's step quickened.

CHAPTER
THREE

It was stuffy in the saloon. The beer Gil had ordered was flat, and lukewarm. He had been tempted to have a glass of whisky; he felt the need of it — but the warning Tom Ash had whispered was still in his mind, and so he had settled for beer.

The Swallowfork riders had carried their drinks to a table in the back of the narrow room, Gil with them. Still a Swallowfork rider, though not a Swallowfork rider. And at the table there was little talk. Two men standing at the bar were laughing at something the bartender had said. Gil would rather have been at the bar. He liked a joke when he came to town. He liked to let down with his drinking, but to let down didn't seem to fit the pattern of the men he was with. It was one of the things he hadn't liked about Swallowfork.

Across from him, Colin tossed off a drink of whisky, shuddered, poured another, and then stared at Gil, his dark eyes scowling, and angry. Perspiration streaked his face and plastered his shirt to his shoulders. His hair was black and curly. Without the scowl he would have been rather good looking.

"I hope we're not stuck here too long," Frank Mills growled. "I'm hungry."

"You're always hungry," Gorman said.

But no one laughed.

A tall, wide-shouldered man entered the room, bellied up to the bar and ordered a drink. He had a booming voice to match Brewster's. Several Swallowfork riders turned to look at him.

"That's Max Sidwell," said Mills. "Supposing the rustler we caught had named Sidwell as the man who had hired him?"

"I wish he had," Colin said sharply.

"You're thinking of Jean Rogers, the girl at the hotel," Mills said.

"Shut up," Colin snapped. "Who asked you to say anything?"

"Jean's a nice girl," Mills said. "A really nice girl."

Colin glared at the fat man and it occurred to Gil Daly to wonder if Mills was deliberately baiting Dan Brewster's son. This talk underlined another thing, too. It emphasized how hopeless it was to analyze a situation without a full knowledge of the people involved. Logan, who was supposed to have hired the rustler, remained only a name to him. He didn't know whether or not it would be like Logan to hire some rustling done. Sidwell was a name and nothing more. Jean Rogers, he could guess, was a girl Colin was interested in. And perhaps Max Sidwell also was interested in her, but that was another guess. Aside from the Swallowfork, he didn't know anything about the people in or around Antioch.

And he didn't know the men on Swallowfork, though he had formed some superficial opinions of them. He could sense the drive of Dan Brewster, but didn't know what caused it. He didn't know the deeper things. He didn't know, for instance, why Colin should laugh at the sight of a strangling rustler, and a few moments later turn sick. He didn't know which man was the real Colin — the hard image of his father or a weak and empty shell.

The door to the saloon opened and Dan Brewster came in. He directed a glance toward the table in the rear, and another at Sidwell, to whom he nodded without speaking. Then he stepped to the bar.

"My bottle, Rocky," he said to the man behind it.

The bartender set out a bottle and glass which Brewster carried to the back table. There was a general shifting to make room for him. Several Swallowfork riders murmured a greeting. Brewster sat down. He poured his drink, gulped it, and wiped his mouth with the back of his hand. Then he said, "I saw the sheriff. He's not very happy about what happened."

"Why would he be?" Frank Mills said. "Huggins is lazy."

Brewster shugged his shoulders. Glancing around the table, he seemed to notice Gil Daly for the first time.

"Still waiting around for your money, huh?" he asked slowly.

Gil came to his feet. "That's right."

The owner of Swallowfork reached into his pocket, pulled out some money, selected a ten dollar bill and held it toward Gil. Gil took it.

"I understand you're riding on," Brewster said.

It was on the tip of Gil's tongue to say he wasn't but the hard and steady look in Brewster's eyes warned him not to.

"What else is there to do?" he asked bleakly.

"Nothing," said Brewster, and the word slapped like a bullet. "Nothing. You've got until sundown to get on your way."

Gil could feel a flush of color burning in his face. He pulled in a deep breath, aware of the sharp tightening of his muscles. Here was something he couldn't take, but something he had to take. Here was a time to crawl.

"Frank," Brewster said, "and Gorman. Keep an eye on him. See that he doesn't get lost on the way out of town."

Gil stared at the two men Brewster had named, then swung around and moved toward the door, still feeling his anger. He noticed Max Sidwell looking at him thoughtfully, and he wondered how much of what had been said was loud enough for Sidwell to hear. But it really wasn't important. He came to the saloon door, thrust it open, and stepped out into the sultry heat of the afternoon. He crossed the street, then stopped, suddenly angry with himself.

What was the matter with him? He wasn't crawling. The decision to quit Swallowfork had been his own. He had made it, and then in effect, Brewster had said he was fired. The decision to ride on was his own. He had made it, then Brewster had ordered him to ride on. Stripped of its bluster what Brewster had said had no real meaning. He could take offense if he wanted to. He could strike back if he wanted to. But for what reason? What would it prove if he did?

Frank Mills and Slim Gorman had left the saloon and were crossing the street toward him. Gorman, tall and slightly stooped, and scowling. Mills taking two steps to Gorman's one and looking unhappy about this assignment. Probably thinking of the steak he had promised himself at the Antioch House.

"The corral's down the street," Gorman said as they came up.

"I know it," Gil said. "But I've got some things to buy. I want some supper. It's still an hour more until sundown."

"You'd better not wait for sundown," Gorman said flatly.

"I'm in no hurry," Gil said. "What are you going to do about it?"

He stood on the board walk, slightly above the two men in the street. He had a distinct advantage. If Gorman clawed for his gun he would have to whip it high. Gil had only to tilt his holster. And he had another advantage. To these men he was an unknown quantity. They knew nothing of his proficiency, or lack of it. Brewster had labeled him a saddle bum, but many a saddle bum had been made so by his guns.

Gorman's face darkened. His right hand brushed back close to his holster. He took a quick glance at Frank Mills.

"Sundown," Mills said. "There's no rush. Brewster said sundown."

30

Gil chuckled, feeling the lift of this small victory. He started down the street, turning into the Emporium when he reached it.

Ollie Schmidt boasted that you could buy anything at the Emporium, and that if you couldn't find what you wanted, he would order it for you. Chiefly, the Emporium was three stores in one: groceries, hardware and dry goods. When Gil walked up to the grocery counter, a group of women occupied the other side of the store, studying the patterns of several bolts of cloth. Ollie was with them.

Gil, hearing the murmur of their voices, glanced that way. He thought, at first, there were two men in the group, but realized almost immediately that the tall, slender figure in jeans and a man's shirt was the figure of a girl. She had draped a length of one of the bolts of cloth over her shoulders and around her waist, and was laughing. Gil heard her ask, "How would this look?"

"It would make a beautiful dress, Myra," said one of the women.

"And you should wear dresses," said another. "You have the figure for it, my dear."

Myra Chenoweth had turned and saw Gil staring at her. The amused smile on her lips vanished.

Gil didn't look away. He nodded his head as though in agreement with what he had heard, and he was close enough to the girl to see the quick, flaming color in her face.

"I believe you have a customer, Ollie," said Myra Chenoweth. "I'm in no hurry. I don't think I like this material."

"It's reasonable," said Ollie Schmidt. "There's no finer dress goods on Fifth Avenue, New York. Think about it a minute."

He left the women and came to wait on Gil. All Gil wanted was some tobacco.

"Tell her to buy the material and wear it made up in a dress," Gil said, chuckling. "I'm only passing through here, but if I saw her in a dress made of that stuff, I'd probably stay."

The storekeeper's eyes twinkled. "I'll tell her."

Gil dropped the tobacco he had purchased into his pocket. He accepted the change Ollie handed him, then took another look toward the group of women. Myra now had her back to him. She had black hair, braided and coiled around her head, a good breadth of shoulders, and a narrow waist. Gil imagined she was almost as tall as he was, and almost as old.

She's probably married, too, he grumbled to himself as he moved toward the door.

Outside, Frank Mills and Slim Gorman were waiting, standing at the edge of the board walk. They didn't speak to him and Gil only glanced at them before he turned on down the street toward the Antioch House. He passed through the hotel's narrow lobby to the restaurant and took a table near the window. There were several others in the room, but no one he knew.

A girl came to the table to take his order. She was young. She had a friendly smile and clear blue eyes. Her light hair was twisted into a loose, low bun on the back of her neck. Faint freckles bridged her nose.

32

"You must be Jean Rogers," Gil said, remembering Frank Mills' mention of that name in the saloon.

"Jean it is," said the girl. "But you're new here."

"Just riding through," Gil said. "I've been at it a week, though."

"That's a long time to be just riding through a place."

"But that's the way it happened. I hear they have good steaks at Antioch House."

The girl didn't answer. She straightened and stared through the window. Gil glanced that way too. There were several men visible but the only ones he knew were Gorman and Colin Brewster. Gorman and Colin were across the street and as he stared at them, Colin broke away and started in the direction of the livery stable. He looked up at Jean. The girl's head was turning as she followed him with her eyes. And her smile was gone. She was frowning.

"About that steak," Gil said.

"Oh, I'm sorry," Jean answered. "Yes, sir. A steak."

She hurried away.

Gil rolled a cigaret and lit it. He saw Frank Mills enter the restaurant and sit at another table. He wasn't surprised. His delay in leaving Antioch apparently fitted in with the desires of the chunky foreman at Swallowfork, who had been looking forward to his dinner. Mills could have his steak and watch him from in here. Gorman would stand guard on the street.

"Suppose I did want to stay here for a while," Gil muttered. "If I wanted to stay, but didn't, I'd be crawling."

He ran his fingers through his hair, the hair which needed cutting. He stared through the window again. Gorman had disappeared. The shadows were longer. He had half an hour before sundown. Maybe forty-five minutes.

"Mind if I join you?" asked a voice at his shoulder.

Gil looked up and recognized Max Sidwell, the tall, broad-shouldered man who had been pointed out to him in the Teton Saloon. Sidwell, at a guess, was about thirty. He had big hands, thick wrists, a pleasant grin.

"Suit yourself," Gil said.

Sidwell took the place next to him. "It isn't often I'm asked to eat with a Swallowfork rider, but then —"

"But then I'm not a Swallowfork rider any more," Gil finished. "You knew that, didn't you?"

"I guessed it. Mind if I ask way?"

"Supposing I said I didn't fit Swallowfork standards."

"That might be a compliment. Looking for another job?"

Gil shook his head.

"As bad as that, huh?"

Gil Daly scowled. Sidwell was reading him too plainly. He said, irrationally. "No, not as bad as that," and was glad when Jean came up just then to take Sidwell's order. Staring once more through the window he listened to their conversation.

"Hello, Max."

"Howdy, Jean."

"I didn't know you were coming to town today."

"I didn't either. This trip is an extra."

The girl's voice lowered. "He's here, Max."

34

"I know it," said Max.

"You promised me —"

"I'll be leaving early."

They went on talking in half-whispers, but Gil's attention now centered on Dan Brewster, who had come in sight across the street from the direction of the livery stable. He was carrying a heavy canvas sack in his hand, and as Gil watched he turned into a door marked, LAND SALES — CATTLE SALES — ASSAY OFFICE. He returned to the street empty handed.

Jean finished her conversation with Max Sidwell and left the table. Gil looked toward the man who had joined him and said, "Tell me about the Tetons. Is there much gold found there?"

"Not much," Sidwell answered. "I suppose there's plenty of gold there as some folks are always looking for it. But there's never been a really big strike."

"There's an assay office across the street."

"It's mainly a land and cattle office. Kemp does a little assay work when someone asks him to."

"Did you ever hear of a man named Ed Farley?"

Sidwell frowned. He was silent for a moment. Then he shook his head. "Can't say as I have."

"Or Pete Enders?"

"Sure. Everyone knows old Pete. He's been working the Tetons for years, sometimes alone, but he'll take anyone with him who will go. He's a cross, stubborn man, hard to get along with. He's got a daughter here in town who does sewing. Her husband's dead. Pete comes to see her occasionally. He's always talking about what he's going to do for her. Maybe he will do something some day. Stranger things have happened. You're not thinking of going prospecting with Pete Enders, are you?"

"Could I find him?"

"If he's off in the Tetons, I doubt it."

Jean Rogers brought their food and they started eating. Gil now and then glanced through the window toward the assay office, fitting into a loose picture what he knew and what he could guess and what Max Sidwell had told him. Two Swallowfork riders had caught a man on a lame horse, riding a trail left by a herd of rustled cattle. They had assumed he was one of the rustlers, who had dropped behind when his horse went lame. The man, himself, had insisted he had been in the Tetons with Pete Enders, prospecting. There actually was a prospector named Pete Enders who, whenever he could, took someone with him on his trips.

The rustler had stuck to his story almost to the end. At the end, perhaps in the hope of saving his life, he had admitted Brewster's charges. But after his death, the ore samples he said he was carrying, had been found in his saddlebags. Brewster had brought them with him to town. They were now at the assay office. Brewster had insisted they were only rocks — but supposing they weren't? Supposing the first story the rustler had told had been true?

Gil, still watching the street, saw the door to the assay office open. A man stepped out on the walk. A stoop-shouldered man in his shirt sleeves, wearing an eyeshade and carrying a piece of paper. The man looked up and down the street, then hurried from sight in the direction of the Teton Saloon. Gil caught his breath. He thought, maybe the assay showed something. Maybe the old prospector's hit it at last.

Sidwell finished his meal and pushed back his chair.

"About that job," he suggested. "Anyone can tell you how to get to my place. Max Sidwell's."

"You mean that?" Gil asked.

"Of course I do."

"I'll think it over," Gil promised.

He watched Sidwell leave the room, then glanced around toward the table at which Frank Mills had been sitting. Mills was gone. And there was something strange about that. Mills loved his food. He didn't hurry it. He should still have been here, but something had called him away. An explanation for that came to Gil's mind. When Brewster questioned the rustler he had asked who hired him: Sidwell or Logan? To the Swallowfork, in all probability, Sidwell fell into the same classification as Logan. Wherefore, there was a good chance that Mills wouldn't appreciate the fact that he had sat next to Sidwell, here in this restaurant, and that they had talked to each other. There was a good chance that no one on Swallowfork would appreciate it.

Under the screen of the table, Gil loosened the gun in his holster. He pulled in a long, slow breath. The sudden moisture of perspiration chilled his forehead. He tried to tell himself that he was imagining a danger, but every bit of conviction he possessed leaned the other way. He stared through the window. The sun, now almost down, threw long shadows across the dust of the street. Gorman was in sight again, and with him, Frank Mills. But no one else. No other Swallowfork riders.

They told me I had until sundown, Gil thought. They probably meant it. Nothing's going to happen.

He got to his feet. He left money on the table to pay for his food, then headed for the lobby. He walked through the lobby to the door. Outside, he turned toward the livery stable. Across the street, Gorman and Frank Mills moved that way also. A shiver ran up and down Gil's back. There were few people in sight. Ahead of him he could see no one at all.

I'll get my horse and ride, he told himself. That's what they want.

But he wasn't sure it was going to be as simple as that.

The yard in front of the livery stable was empty. The barn door stood slightly open. Gil approached it, calling, "Hey, Tarbow! Tarbow!" The door opened wider. Two men stepped out, but Tarbow wasn't one of them. The two were Colin and Hank Morse.

Morse was holding the gun, holding it to cover Gil Daly.

Gil came to an abrupt stop. Without turning his head he knew that Frank Mills and Slim Gorman were closing in behind him, probably spread out so as not to stand in Hank's line of fire. He recalled the whispered advice that Tom Ash had given him, the warning to make a break for it. But it was too late for that now. He had no chance even to go for his gun. Hank Morse was too close to miss. Colin was even closer, tight-lipped, scowling, both fists clenched.

"What do you want?" Gil heard himself asking. "Brewster said —"

"Brewster's not running this little show," Colin broke in. "This is my idea. Frank, get his gun."

Gil moistened his lips. He heard someone step up behind him and felt the tug as his gun was pulled from its holster. He stared at Colin, amazed at the blazing anger in Colin's face. Right now, Colin was living in his father's image. He wasn't behind a screen of shrubbery, heaving his breakfast. He had cast off such weakness. He radiated violence.

"Your idea?" Gil said slowly.

"Yeah, my idea," said Colin. "We want to give you something to remember Swallowfork by. A going away present. Like this."

He stepped closer. His clenched fist swept up at Gil's face and all the weight of his body was in the blow. Gil rocked backward, thrusting out his arm. Colin's knuckles barely grazed his cheek. But the man's other fist caught him in the stomach, doubling him over. He straightened. He forgot momentarily about the other men here. Colin outweighed him by at least thirty pounds, was taller and had a longer reach. In a stand-up, slugging match, he would have little chance against Colin, but in close he could to some extent equalize the difference. He ripped a blow at Colin's stomach and followed this with another. He shot his fist at Colin's jaw and then two more blows to the stomach. He hunched over, boring in, and the blows Colin was raining at him glanced off the side of his head and his shoulders and arms.

So this was Colin's show, was it? Yeah — Colin's payment to him for what he had witnessed behind the screen of shrubbery on Squaw Creek. Well, he would make the payment costly. He slammed his fists again at Colin's stomach and as the man stumbled backward, aimed a blow at his jaw. It never landed. Pain exploded in Gil's head. Bright flecks of light danced in front of his eyes. His knees suddenly folded and he plunged to the ground and there was no strength in him to move again. From what seemed like a great distance away he heard Colin swearing bitterly at Frank Mills, and he realized, vaguely, what had happened. Mills had stepped up behind him and slammed him over the head, probably with a gun.

The wrangle between Mills and Colin went on, but Gil heard little of it. Waves of darkness were sweeping over him. He tried to fight them off. The voices he had heard faded out, then came again.

"What do we do with him now, Frank?" someone asked, and it sounded like Gorman.

"Throw some water on him," Frank Mills said. "Then load him on his horse and get him started up the road."

And then Gorman again: "You're riding Colin pretty hard, Frank. He wasn't whipped when you stopped it."

"Wasn't he?" Frank Mills chuckled. "I know what I'm doing, Slim. Leave Colin to me."

CHAPTER
FOUR

Myra Chenoweth had supper with her father at the Antioch House. Afterward, they mounted their horses for the long ride home. It was fully dark, now, but in another hour the moon would be up. There was a light breeze and a promise in the soft air that it would be a pleasant evening.

"You're sure you've finished all your errands?" Sam Chenoweth asked.

"I didn't have many," Myra said.

"And you've seen everyone you wanted to see?"

The girl nodded.

"Max Sidwell was in town," Sam said mildly. "I always liked Max."

"And Max is interested only in Jean Rogers," said Myra, her eyes twinkling. "Must you keep on trying to find me a husband?"

"A girl your age ought to be married," Sam grumbled.

"What would you do at the ranch without me?"

"Mother and I would get along."

"But you'd have to hire a man to take my place."

"We could afford it."

"How?"

"We'd manage, somehow."

Myra laughed pleasantly. "Dad, quit worrying about me. I'll probably find a man, someday."

"You could have any man you want." Sam snorted. "You're just too particular."

They passed the livery stable. At the sound of a shot, both reined up and looked back. They sat tensely in their saddles, awaiting the sound of an answering shot. But none came.

"I wonder what that was about?" Sam said, frowning.

"It didn't sound like it was in town," Myra said. "It seemed to come from over there." She pointed to the left, to the clustering houses behind the main street. "I wonder —" Her voice trailed off uneasily.

"You wonder what?"

"Max Sidwell was in town. So was Colin Brewster. But — but Jean said Max promised to keep out of Colin's way."

"So it's like that, huh?"

"When Jean first came here she went out some with Colin. Then she met Max and fell in love with him. But Colin was a hard man to drop."

"You had no difficulty dropping him," Sam pointed out.

"Or his father either," Myra said.

Sam Chenoweth jerked around to stare at his daughter. "What's this about Colin's father? I never heard you mention it before. If Dan Brewster —"

"Forget it, Dad. It's all over. It was never very serious. I shouldn't have brought it up."

42

But the scowl which had come to Sam Chenoweth's face stayed there. He kept looking at his daughter as though expecting her to add something more. When she didn't, he said, half irritably, "You ought to tell me about things like that. I've got a right to know."

"Would it have made any difference in your attitude toward Brewster?" Myra asked.

Sam Chenoweth shrugged his shoulders. He glanced back along the main steet and Myra looked that way, too. There was no sign of excitement anywhere. "It was probably just a stray shot we heard," Sam muttered.

Myra nodded and they rode on, out of town, across the Rhymer River bridge, and then along the road which followed it for the next dozen miles. Where the Rhymer River flowed out of the Swallowfork basin was another bridge, and from there the road north followed the deep gully of Four Mile Creek, twisting along above it.

After the moon came up they rode faster, though not with any particular haste. They crossed the second Rhymer River bridge and climbed their horses to the Four Mile Creek road. Some little distance along it they sighted a lone rider. Instinctively, both slowed down, wondering who the man was. And together, they made the same discovery.

"Something's wrong up there," Sam said, glancing at his daughter.

"Or maybe the man's drunk," Myra answered.

The horse ahead of them was walking. The man in the saddle reeled from side to side. His body was slumped forward. And he didn't raise up or greet them as they joined him. He showed no awareness of their presence.

Myra caught her breath. "Dad," she whispered. "Dad, his head."

"I see it," Sam Chenoweth said.

He reached for the horse's bridle and pulled the horse to a stop. The man in the saddle seemed to try to straighten up. His shoulders lifted. The entire left side of his face was bloodstreaked from the open wound in his scalp. His lips moved in an attempt to say something. He seemed to look straight at Myra but she was sure he didn't see her. He started to lean sideways.

Myra slipped out of her saddle. She caught his body as it pitched toward the ground. She broke his fall, but she went down with him.

"Now that was a pretty sight," Sam said, dismounting and helping her to her feet.

"Dad, what are we going to do with him?" Myra asked. "He's bled terribly from that cut in his head."

"So much he's about out, I reckon," Sam answered. "But we can probably get him on to the ranch. Who do you reckon he is?"

Myra bent over the figure on the ground. The man was young and had light hair and there was something familiar in his features. In a moment she had it. This was the man who had come into the Emporium this afternoon while she was looking at some dress goods. He had sent her some impertinent message through Ollie Schmidt . . . though perhaps he hadn't meant it as impertinent.

"I saw him today in the Emporium," she said, looking up at her father. "I think he was just riding through the country. How do you suppose he was hurt?"

44

"Maybe he can tell us in the morning," Sam Chenoweth said. "We'll prop him up, then I'll pull him into the saddle. You boost. I'll ride the rest of the way behind him."

Together, they managed it.

Gil Daly awoke to the realization of a hammering pain in his head. He raised his hands and touched a bandage. The sudden memory of what had happened, came back to him. There had been a fight in the yard in front of the corral in Antioch. Frank Mills had ended it, slashing him over the head. Some time after that, he had been helped to mount his horse, and for hours, it had seemed, he had clung precariously to the saddle. There had been a man riding with him for a time, and then he was alone. Where he was now he couldn't guess, unless at some ranch along the way.

Sunlight was streaming in through the window. The air carried the smell of bacon and coffee, and the smell was good. There were sheets on the bed he was in, clean, white sheets. Over the top sheet lay a patchwork quilt, tied with red yarn. From some other part of the house he heard footsteps and then the sound of someone humming. A woman humming. The footsteps moved to the door of his room. The humming ceased. Then, very quietly, the door opened and a woman looked in. She had gray hair and a round, pleasant face. Her brown eyes twinkled at him.

"So you're awake. And I'll wager you're hungry. What a fuss they made over you last night. Myra was all for riding back to Antioch for a doctor. I'll admit you looked as though you needed one."

The door was wide open now and the woman was coming into the room. She was short and chunky. She laid a soft, cool hand on Gil's forehead. "Not much fever," she decided. "How do bacon and eggs sound with maybe some potatoes and, of course, coffee."

"It would be wonderful," Gil said.

"I'm Kathy Chenoweth," said the woman.

"And I'm Gil Daly."

"That doesn't tell me much."

"I'm afraid there isn't much to add."

"Maybe, then, we've got a sensible man on our hands," said the woman. "I'll get you some breakfast. Pretty soon, if I'm any judge, my daughter will be back and start firing questions at you. It might be wise to fortify yourself."

She left the room, left Gil chuckling, left him with the conviction that he was going to like her no matter what her daughter might ask.

It was mid-morning before Myra came in. Gil was feeling better, stronger. He was sitting up in the bed. The painful hammering in his head was still there, but not so intense. There was a gash in his skull almost three inches long, Kathy Chenoweth had told him. It had been washed out, part of his hair had been chopped away, and the edges of the gash had been pressed together. This explained the reason for the tight bandage.

Gil recognized Myra the minute she appeared in the doorway. She was wearing the same clothing he had seen the day before: blue jeans and a man's blue shirt.

46

It was open at the throat — a sun-tanned throat — and her face and the backs of her hands were deeply tanned. Her forehead bore the mark of the sweat band of her hat, a man's high crowned hat which she held.

"This is Myra," said Kathy Chenoweth, joining her in the doorway. "Sam and I make a mistake with her. We should have ordered a boy."

Myra shrugged her shoulders as though used to hearing something like this. She can on into the room, showing a slight frown. Her eyes were brown, steady.

"We were worried about you last night," she said slowly. "This morning, you seem much better."

"I feel a little shaky," Gil said. "That's all. Who brought me here?"

"Father and I. We found you on the road above Four Mile Creek."

"How does a person thank someone for a thing like that?"

Myra again shrugged her shoulders. "Do you want to tell me what happened?"

"Someone struck me over the head," Gil said.

"Someone?"

"It feels that way. That must have been what happened."

The girl's lips tightened as though she had expected more, some story she could understand. "That's all you have to say?"

"Suppose I named the man who struck me," Gil said. "Suppose he was a friend of yours and what I said about him was pretty bad. Would you believe me?"

"Probably not."

"But if he was an enemy, you would."

"I might."

"Of course, anything I said could easily be untrue."

A look of irritation crossed the girl's face. "Are you trying to make a game of this? What do you mean?"

"Maybe he means he doesn't want to talk about what happened," Kathy Chenoweth said from the door. "Sometimes people don't. I recall one time when you came home from town, angry and crying. When we asked you what had happened, neither your father or I could get a word out of you."

The girl looked quickly at her mother, then back at Gil. Her eyes were angry. A flush had deepened the color of her skin. She turned abruptly toward the door. Kathy Chenoweth stood aside to let her leave the room, then came back inside.

"There's nothing like curiosity to get a girl all riled up," she observed.

"And are you curious," Gil asked.

"I'm dying of it."

"Maybe I'm not proud of the story I'd have to tell, if I told the truth."

"I've never met a man who was a hero every day of his life," Kathy Chenoweth said. "I reckon everyone's entitled to a few dark corners. The important thing is to be stronger more often than you're weak."

Gil Daly tested his legs during the afternoon, and by evening felt able to sit at the supper table with the Chenoweths. Sam, at the head of the table, said grace in a low, rumbling voice, and then carved the roast which had filled the house with such a good smell in the late afternoon hours. Gil was across the table from Myra. She had ridden in just before suppertime and had changed from jeans and shirt to a dress with a pink flowery pattern. He didn't know that this was unusual.

There was casual talk during the meal. Ranch talk. Sam mentioned a drift fence which was down and which he would start work on the next day. Myra said the south well was running better and that more of their cattle could be shifted to the south meadow. Then, over their coffee, Myra glanced at her father and said, "I saw Joe Broomfield this afternoon. He told me that Swallowfork had fired a man they hired just a week ago. You were talking of hiring a man, Dad. If we could locate this man the Swallowfork fired, he might come to work for us. But I suppose we wouldn't want a man fired by Swallowfork." She looked quickly at Gil.

"That all depends," said Sam Chenoweth.

"On what?" Myra demanded. "As I understand it, this man the Swallowfork hired and then fired, was just a saddle bum."

"What's a saddle bum?" Gil inquired softly.

Myra looked straight at him. "Don't you know? A drifter. A man who never stays put. A man who's always just passing through the country."

"Some drifters," Kathy Chenoweth said, "make pretty good men when a woman steadies them down. I know a saddle bum who turned out pretty well."

"Now look here, Kathy!" Sam scowled at his wife. "I wasn't a saddle bum. You can't say —"

"Weren't you just drifting through when you met me?" Kathy asked, smiling.

"I was looking for a job. Looking for a job doesn't make a man a bum."

The grin on Gil Daly's face couldn't have been broader. He watchd Myra but she wouldn't look at him. She was staring at her coffee, biting her lips.

"Another thing," said Sam Chenoweth. "When the Swallowfork rode into town the other day, they brought along the body of a rustler they'd shot. Maybe this saddle bum they fired didn't have the stomach to ride with Swallowfork, to face what he saw coming. Maybe he didn't want any part in a cattle war — if that's what we've got ahead of us. Maybe he just wanted a job on a ranch, looking after cattle."

Myra's head lifted. She stared at her father.

"Can I say something?" Gil asked.

"You don't have to," Kathy told him. "They've both figured it out. You're the saddle bum they're talking about. Did you quit Swallowfork, or were you fired?"

"It depends on how you look at it."

"Things usually do."

Myra got up as though to leave the table, then sat down again, determined to see this through. The flush was still on her face.

Sam Chenoweth cleared his throat. He said, "Gil, you don't have to answer this — but can you tell me anything about the rustler the Swallowfork brought in?"

Gil shook his head. "I'd rather not. You live here. My ideas on what happened might be wrong."

"What about that cut on your head?"

50

"I was given until sundown to leave town," Gil said slowly. "Maybe I wasn't prompt enough."

"Until sundown to leave town," Sam Chenoweth repeated. "At a guess, Brewster didn't want you hanging around. He didn't want you to talk."

"Or didn't like the color of my hair."

Sam Chenoweth grunted. He reached for his pipe and loaded it and started smoking. "I had a talk with the sheriff before I left town," he said after a moment. "The sheriff, Carl Huggins, is a good man. A little slow, maybe. A little cautious. But no one runs over him. He said Brewster had told him the rustler admitted working for Howard Logan. I've known Logan better than ten years. I don't believe it. I don't think Huggins believed the story either. Kathy, bring me a piece of paper and a pencil."

Kathy left the table. Sam Chenoweth cleared a place in front of him, then started drawing. Gil finished his coffee. He glanced across the table at Myra but the girl still wouldn't meet his eyes.

"Look here," Sam said finally. "I've drawn sort of a map of the upper Rhymer River valley. It'll help explain things."

Gil moved to the head of the table and stood looking over Sam Chenoweth's shoulder at the map the man had drawn. He noticed the position of Antioch and of the Swallowfork basin, half surrounded by the foothills of the Toltec Mountains. He saw Logan's ranch. Max Sidwell's, Joe Broomfield's, Charlie Weseloh's, and the Chenoweth ranch, where he was now. The area of the

Swallowfork was as large as most of the others combined.

"North and west of Antioch," Sam Chenoweth said, "there's only one large outfit. The Swallowfork. Dan Brewster's got the best land. He's got the water. The rest of us are just sort of hanging on. I don't mean some of us don't make a living, but when times are tough we barely get by. It would be easier on us if we got the water we're entitled to from the Rhymer River and the other streams which cross the Swallowfork basin. One of our troubles is that we don't. A few years ago, Brewster dammed the streams which cross the basin. We took the matter to court and beat him. He had to blow up his dams, but that didn't end the matter. There's a dozen places across the basin where the streams can be diverted. Each time that happens, the new dry land which the streams cross, soak it up and give Brewster new, grass-rich meadows." Chenoweth grunted. "Know what he calls the diversion of the streams? Act of God! He's playing God, all right, himself."

"You can't stop him?"

"We haven't been able to. Men who ride into the basin to find out why a stream has almost run dry, get shot at. The excuse is this rumor of rustling. Brewster claims he's losing cattle. My inference, he's blamed everyone whose land borders on his. He's never proved a case. I don't think he ever will. He doesn't need all the water he uses. He's bitter about the court decision against him. One of these days —" Sam shook his head.

"What's going to happen one of these days" Gil asked.

"One of these days, some of the men around Swallowfork are going to ride into the basin and blow it sky high."

"Sam," Kathy said sharply.

Sam sighed. "Maybe I won't be with them. Or maybe I will. It all depends on what happens. Let's go out on the porch. The evenings are nice."

Sam Chenoweth and Gil Daly moved out on the porch. Gil rolled a cigaret, recalling the details of the map, verifying Sam's story with what he had heard while on the Swallowfork. There had been talk of flooding the east meadow. He had asked what was meant, and Frank Mills had said, grinning, *The Rhymer River is as fickle as a woman. With a little encouragement, it'll run where we want it to run.*

"A man can just take so much," Sam muttered. "There comes a day when he's got to hit back. Dan Brewster doesn't realize that. Dan's changed. There was a time when we didn't have this threat of trouble."

"When did he change?" Gil asked.

"I don't know. It was gradual like, I suppose. It was —"

He broke off, straightened, and then got to his feet, his hand brushing back his coat to touch his gun. Gil heard a rider approaching. He thought, This is what happens in a country when there's trouble ahead. You keep a gun handy.

"Sam!" called a man reining up in the yard. "Hey, Sam. It's Charlie Weseloh."

"I'm on the porch, Charlie."

The man rode closer. It was still quite dark. The moon hadn't come up. Gil couldn't distinguish the man's features and he was quite sure Weseloh couldn't see him.

"A cup of coffee, Charlie?" Kathy asked from the doorway.

"Not tonight," the man answered.

Kathy hesitated, then turned back. After she had gone Weseloh lowered his voice. "Sam, did you hear about the murder in Antioch last night?"

"Murder?"

"You couldn't name it anything else. Someone got Bill Kemp. Called him to the door of his house about seven-thirty. A couple minutes later his wife heard a shot. When she looked outside Bill was lying on the walk near the porch steps."

"That must have been the shot Myra and I heard as we were leaving town," Sam said. "But Bill Kemp? Who had it in for Bill Kemp?"

"Maybe someone he rooked in a land or cattle deal. Or maybe someone else. Maybe someone who wanted his wife. Helen Kemp isn't a bad looker."

Weseloh chuckled over that remark.

"What does the sheriff think?" Sam asked.

"I don't know. He didn't arrest anyone last night, and early this morning he left for Swallowfork to look into some charges of rustling. I think some day I'm going to snag some Swallowfork cattle. I might as well. I'm one of the men always getting blamed for it."

The two men talked for a while longer, but Gil paid little attention. He was thinking along a line of his own. Ore samples had been found in the saddlebags of the man the Swallowfork had lynched. Brewster had brought the ore to town and had taken it to Kemp's office. He had left at once. A few minutes later a man had stepped from the office a paper in his hand, a man who looked excited and who probably was Bill Kemp. And that night, Bill Kemp had been called to his door and murdered.

Gil could make a very obvious deduction. The ore samples hadn't been just rocks. They had indicated a worth-while discovery. Kemp must have made his report to Brewster and Brewster, in all probability, had asked him to keep it quiet. Then, after dark, had made sure of Kemp's silence. This was pure guess work, but it hung together. It made sense.

Sam and Charlie Weseloh finished their talk and Weseloh rode on. Then, after a time, Sam said, "Gil, you're awful quiet. What are you thinking?"

"Nothing," Gil said.

But that wasn't true. He was thinking of the old prospector over in the Tetons who had made a gold strike, but didn't know it, and wouldn't hear of the results of Kemp's assay. He was thinking of how long he had worked to save the money to buy his ranch, and of how quickly he had gone broke. He was thinking of the wasted year since then, and of how many more years it would take to save up the money to get started again.

He was thinking of a possible short-cut.

CHAPTER
FIVE

Gil slept soundly that night. He had a late breakfast in the Chenoweth kitchen which Kathy Chenoweth fixed for him. Afterward she insisted on changing the bandage on his head, and reported the wound healing nicely. "But you ought to take it easy," she advised. "Stay here for another day."

"A saddle bum always rides on," Gil insisted. "He never stays anywhere very long."

The woman smiled. "I believe Myra will have something to say to you when she rides in. An apology comes hard to a girl like Myra."

"One isn't needed," said Gil. "I've had eight jobs in the past year."

"And before that?"

"Before that, I had a place of my own. Not a large place, not a large herd. But I went broke awfully quickly."

"The last few years haven't been easy on anyone in the cattle business. But prices are picking up."

"Too late," Gil said, scowling. "And to save up the money to start again would take too long on a cow hand's wages."

"You could rob a bank."

Gil chuckled. "I'm thinking of that."

"Or you could marry some nice girl whose father owns a ranch."

"Myra?" said Gil Daly, still chuckling.

"If she would have you, but she won't. I sometimes wonder if any man will ever measure up to what Myra wants, or if Myra knows what she wants."

Toward noon, Myra rode into the yard. She swung from the saddle, tied her horse to the corral fence, and came toward the house, pulling off her hat and brushing the dust from her shoulders and arms. She walked with the free stride of a boy. From a distance, she looked like a slim, lithe boy.

Gil, who had been sitting on the porch, stood up as she climbed the steps. "Another hot day," he said.

"They're all hot, this time of the year," Myra agreed.

She stopped, then turned from the door and came toward him. She sat down in the chair next to his, leaning back, crossing her legs in front of her, and dropping her hat to the porch floor. She was staring ahead, frowning.

"I was pretty blunt in what I said last night, wasn't I?"

"Not too blunt," Gil said.

"Dad's been looking for a man we could put on. The work's not too hard."

"You're offering me the job?"

"If you want it."

Gil shook his head. "You're forgetting something. Swallowfork ordered me out of the country."

The girl straightened. She reached for her hat and stood up and turned to face him. The scorn in her eyes was something Gil could almost feel.

"So I was right last night," she said sharply. "A saddle bum."

Gil raised a lazy eyebrow.

Without another word, Myra Chenoweth strode through the open door. She didn't speak to him at dinner. She didn't look at him either. And as soon as dinner was over, she hurried away.

Sam Chenoweth hadn't come back to the ranch, and wouldn't until suppertime, Kathy told Gil. And then she asked, "What happened between you and Myra?"

"She offered me a job," Gil said. "I turned it down."

"Then you're riding on?"

He nodded.

"Somehow or other," Kathy said, "I didn't think you would."

She seemed disappointed. The sparkle had gone from her eyes.

Gil went out to the corral, caught and saddled his horse, and then returned to the house to thank Kathy Chenoweth for what she had done. But the woman only murmured a brief reply, and as he rode away, Gil knew she was watching him.

I could have told her I wasn't exactly riding on, he reflected. But she would have asked questions. She would have wanted to know why.

He shook his head. It was better this way.

At the road above Four Mile Creek, Gil pulled up and rolled and lit a cigaret. To his right, to the north, was the way out of the valley. To the south was Antioch. He turned toward Antioch, hoping he wouldn't run into any of the Swallowfork riders, either on the road or when he got to town.

Dan Brewster paced back and forth in the living room of the Swallowfork ranch house. This had seemed like a cheerful room during the years when his wife lived, and when Colin had been a youngster, growing up. But it didn't seem cheerful tonight and it hadn't for a long time. It was clean. Frank Mills' wife kept it clean, fussing at him about any cigar ashes dropped on the floor, or any dirt tracked in. But the room wasn't the same. Maybe it was the silence that made it seem so gloomy. Perhaps, as he had thought occasionally, it needed a woman in it again. A woman who lived and belonged here.

There was a knock on the door. Brewster answered it and admitted Frank Mills. The chunky foreman took off his hat as he always did when he entered the house, mopped a hand over his head, and said, "No sign of him yet, Dan. But I still think he'll make it here tonight. He said he would come here after he had seen Logan.

Mills was speaking of Sheriff Huggins, who had started from Antioch the day before to check the report on the rustling.

"I wish he'd get here," Brewster muttered. "But he won't have done a thing. If the trail of the rustled cattle led straight to Logan's door, he'd try not to see it. We should have headed for Logan's two day ago, ourselves."

"We've got to give him a chance," said Mills. "After all, he's the sheriff. I'll keep a lookout for him."

Brewster shrugged. "Where's Colin?"

"I don't know. He hasn't come in yet."

"When he comes in," Brewster said, "tell him I want to see him."

Mills nodded and left the room, closing the door quietly behind him.

Brewster continued his pacing, chewing the dead stub of his after-supper cigar, and trying to curb his impatience. He didn't quite understand why he hadn't gone ahead and had things out with Logan, two nights ago. When he left the sheriff's office in Antioch after making a report on the rustling, it had been in his mind to ride for Logan's immediately.

But he hadn't. First there had been the matter of the saddle bum he had fired, the problem of running him out of the country. Then, while waiting around to make sure Gil Daly was on his way, he had taken what might have been ore samples in to Kemp, for checking. And he had waited for Kemp's report. He hadn't received it, and now he never would; for that night, Kemp had been murdered.

Brewster spent no time puzzling over the murder of Bill Kemp, whom he hadn't liked anyhow. He was looking at the other developments of the night. Gorman had reported to him that the saddle bum had put up a fight, and that to make sure he was headed out of the valley, Hank Morse had ridden up the road with

60

him. Colin had disappeared for the evening, probably to hang around the girl who worked at the Antioch House restaurant, and with whom he fancied himself in love. And Mills, of all people, had showed up at the Teton Saloon, drunk, Tom Ash with him. By early evening, he hadn't had anyone to ride with him to Logan's.

I suppose it was just as well this way, he told himself. We'll give the sheriff a chance. But if Huggins doesn't act . . .

He smacked his fist into the palm of his hand.

Voices reached him from the yard. A moment later Colin came storming into the room, slamming the door behind him. The twisted scowl, tight and bitter, which was becoming almost habitual on Colin's face, marred it again tonight. He glared at his father.

"What in the hell's the matter with you?" Brewster asked irritably.

"If you want to see me, don't send Mills after me," Colin said. "I can't stand the man, and you know it."

"You don't get along with anyone very well," Brewster told him.

Colin sailed his hat toward the hall tree in the corner of the room. It missed the hooks and fell to the floor. He crossed over, picked it up and hung it. Then he ran his fingers through his hair, thick dark hair, curly and matted with perspiration. He had a high forehead and the same square stubborn jaw as his father.

"What do you want of me?" he growled. And in his voice, it seemed to Brewster, there was the same, sullen, little boy sound which Colin had used years ago in his resentment against discipline.

"I just wondered where you had been?" Brewster said.

"I rode to Antioch, this afternoon, if it's any business of yours."

"To see that girl who works in the hotel restaurant?"

"And what's the matter with Jean Rogers?"

"Why nothing, Colin."

"Then quit nagging me about her."

Brewster took the stub of his cigar from his mouth. He threw it into the fireplace, then glanced around the room, trying to picture Jean Rogers here as Colin's wife. It might be nice, he told himself. It might be just what the house needed. A woman here again, and some children. He nodded his head, but deep in his mind was the conviction that things would never work out that way.

"I've been thinking for a long time you ought to get married," he said slowly.

Colin stiffened. "I'll get married when I want to."

"You don't have to snap my head off," Brewster said.

"Then quit telling me what to do and what not to do."

Anger welled up in Brewster's body, but he held it in check. It was always this way, lately, when he and Colin had a talk. Sooner or later they were shouting at each other. What was the matter with them? It hadn't been like this when Colin's mother was alive. Somewhere, since then, he and Colin had lost touch with each other. Or he might as well face it honestly. Somewhere, he had failed as a father.

Colin reached abruptly for his hat, put it on and started for the door. When he got there and opened it, he looked back. "Aren't you going to ask me where I am going?" he asked sarcastically.

Brewster said nothing. He heard the door slam and once more was alone in the house. Out in the kitchen he poured a cup of coffee from the pot still on the stove, but the coffee was bitter to his taste.

Sheriff Carl Huggins reached the Swallowfork ranch about at hour later. Frank Mills came in with him. Huggins looked tired. His clothing was sweat-stained and dusty. He hadn't shaved for two days. The wrinkles in his thin face seemed deeper. His eyes were webbed with red lines.

"Beth is making some fresh coffee," Mills said, referring to his wife.

Brewster nodded. He had already heard sounds from the kitchen. "How about something stronger than coffee?" he asked the sheriff.

"Not this time," Huggins said. "I've still got a long ride to Antioch."

"You could stay here tonight."

"I've got a problem facing me in Antioch. I shouldn't have left when I did. Dan, who would have killed Bill Kemp?"

"How should I know?"

"It's something I can't figure," said the sheriff. "Bill Kemp was a square shooter. I can't think of anyone who might have hated him. He got along with his wife.

Men like Bill Kemp don't get called to the door and shot down. But that's what happened."

Beth Mills came in with the coffee. She was a colorless, tired looking woman with stringy hair. She served the coffee and then left, only nodding her head at Huggins' word of greeting.

"What about Logan?" Brewster asked when she had gone.

"Let's get to the rustling, first," said the sheriff. "I followed the trail of the cattle you said were rustled, Dan. The trail petered out."

"What do you mean, petered out?"

"Just that. Without leaving your range, the herd broke up, a few head here and there drifting into the hills to the west. There finally wasn't any trail to follow."

"You mean we didn't lost fifty head to the rustlers?"

"Not where I could see."

"That's a damned lie."

The sheriff seemed to take no offense at Brewster's anger. "Go look for yourself, Dan. I followed the trail pointed out to me by Hondo. I could see, at first, where maybe three men had been driving some cattle south. But after a few miles there weren't any signs to follow and the trail left by the riders was gone. Maybe they got scared off. I'm not saying they didn't. I'm not saying an attempt wasn't made to rustle cattle, either. I'm just saying that the trail pointed out to me didn't lead me to Logan's."

"Maybe you didn't want it to."

"Take a look, Dan.

"I don't have to take a look," Dan Brewster shouted. "We caught one of the men. I heard what he said."

Brewster's anger was like a red mist in front of his eyes. His fists clenched. A voice in his mind told him to go easy, that this was what he should have expected, that nothing was to be gained by an open break with the sheriff. But he didn't want to listen.

"Are you telling me the man we brought in wasn't a rustler?" he thundered.

"I'm not saying that yet, Dan," Huggins parried. "But I may say it. The man you killed was Ed Farley. I rode on to see Logan before coming here. Logan tells me that an Ed Farley was with Pete Enders about three months ago when old Pete took off on another of his prospecting trips into the hills."

"A damned convenient lie."

The sheriff finished his coffee and set the cup on the table. "Maybe."

Brewster took a deep breath. "What are you going to do?"

"Find out about Farley."

"And you don't give a damn about the rustling."

"If there was rustling, I do. But so far, I haven't seen that there was any."

Brewster could feel himself calming down. The anger he had felt was still there, but coming under control. He could see very well what lay ahead. Carl Huggins would try to prove Farley hadn't been a rustler. He would have help, of course, from Logan, and from the other vultures sitting on the edge of Swallowfork basin. Sidwell, Bloomfield, Chenoweth and Weseloh. With the sheriff on their side, the vultures would grow bolder. The petty raids they had made on Swallowfork stock would be stepped up. It was time to hit back, and hit back hard.

"So that's it," he said slowly. "That's it."

The sheriff turned to the door. He opened it, then stopped and looked back. He said, "Dan, I don't work for any man. I work by the law. Bring me proof your stock's being rustled, or show me how I can get proof, and not matter who's guilty, I'll throw the man in jail. But don't bring me any more bodies. I wear the star. You don't."

"Get out," Brewster said flatly.

"One thing more," the sheriff said. "Don't start anything with Logan or anyone else. If you do, you'll be the man thrown in jail. That's a promise."

"Get out," Brewster said again.

Carl Huggins mopped his hand over his face. His dark, deep-set eyes looked troubled. He said, "Dan, when you come to town, drop in and see me. Most things can be talked out."

After the sheriff had gone, Frank Mills whistled, then said, "Huggins is sort of feeling his oats, isn't he? I thought for a while you'd mop up the floor with him."

"Maybe I should have," Brewster said. "What did he mean about the trail petering out. I saw the trail myself. I saw which way it led. I heard what Farley told us."

"I suppose we should have gone after Logan two days ago," Mills conceded. "By now, of course, those cattle must have been shoved so far south, we'd never find them."

"But we can still go after Logan."

"Tonight?"

Brewster's impatience was driving him. "Why not?"

Mills shook his head. "I've got another idea."

"What?"

"If we go after Logan, now, and the sheriff denies the rustling, we'll be in a bad spot. We'll have a war on our hands."

"We've got one anyhow."

"Not if we can prove our case. Not if the evidence against the man we go after is foolproof. I know Logan and you do, too. He hates Swallowfork. He just took fifty Swallowfork cattle. He would take fifty more tomorrow if they were handy. Suppose we let him do it, and then hit him. Catch him redhanded. The sheriff couldn't lift a finger against us. No one else could, within the law. A man can always ride after his own cattle."

Dan Brewster's eyes narrowed. He turned this plan over in his mind. He could see its strong points. Right now, on Huggins' false evidence, he had no right to hit at Logan. But if Swallowfork cattle were on Logan's doorstep, no one could blame the Swallowfork for going after them. Going after them hard.

"I'll ride south tonight," Mills was saying. "I'll get Hondo and Crowell. In a day or two, Logan will grab them. When he does, I'll get word back to the ranch. You and the rest of the boys come running."

Brewster nodded. He could wait another day or two, or longer if necessary. And it might be smart to do just that. Shove some cattle close to the line and let Logan grab them. There wasn't a doubt in his mind but that Logan would.

"You use that head of yours sometimes, don't you, Frank," he said, grudgingly.

"Sometimes," Frank Mills agreed.

Brewster studied him. He was grinning. A short and stocky man with a round, ruddy face and clear blue eyes. He was fifty, but didn't look it. He had been on the Swallowfork a dozen years. He knew cattle. He had a way of handling men, of getting a job done. Maybe he rubbed Colin the wrong way but Colin probably needed it.

"How long do you figure it will take?" Brewster asked.

"Two or three days," Mills said. "And let's keep this quiet, Dan. I'll get in touch with you."

Dan Brewster nodded. He felt almost cheerful.

CHAPTER
SIX

Gil Daly had an early supper at the Antioch House restaurant, served to him by Jean Rogers.

"Somehow or other I didn't expect to see you again," she told him, looking curiously at the bandage on his head.

"I'm drifting south, this time," Gil said. "I might even drop in and see Max Sidwell. Any message.

The girl flushed, then laughed and shook her head. "You seem to be picking up a lot of information, in your drifting."

"You do it by asking questions," Gil said. "For instance, what's the name of Peter Enders' daughter?"

"Carrie Hawes. She runs a dressmaking shop up the street."

Gil grinned. "See what I mean?"

"But what use is information like that?"

"Who can tell? Are you sure you haven't a message for Max Sidwell?"

"Not tonight. That is —"

The girl broke off. She was frowning, staring through the window. Her eyes had darkened.

Gil glanced outside. He saw Colin Brewster moving along the walk. Near the Antioch House, Colin hesitated. But he didn't turn in. He walked on.

"Shall I tell Max that Colin's in town?" Gil asked.

"No," the girl said hurriedly. "Please don't —" She turned and hurried away.

Gil finished his meal, went outside, and stood for a moment in front of the Antioch House, staring up the street, hoping he wouldn't run into Colin. Across from the Emporium a crowd had gathered. They were watching the store. Gil wondered why. As he puzzled over this, the door to the Emporium opened and a man stepped out on the walk, a man to attract immediate attention. He was tall and thin, but it was his clothing which caught the eye: high, fancy spurred boots and heavy chaps, an ornamented gun belt and holster, a fringed leather jacket over a white silk shirt, a red handkerchief stiff with starch, and one of the largest hats Gil had ever seen. A hat with a high crown and a wide brim.

He couldn't help but grin. Here were all the obvious marks of a man new to the West, a man with too much money, a dude. Gil could almost hear the jangle of the spurs as the man crossed the walk into the street, strutting, showing off. There were several horses at the tie-rail, one obviously his. The man approached it, grabbed the horn of the saddle with both hands, put a foot in the stirrup, and heaved upward. But he didn't swing astride. Instead, the saddle with its cinch strap loosened, twisted around under the horse, and the weight of the man's body carried him with it. He sprawled ingloriously in the dust.

There were hoots of laughter from most of the watching crowd. There were grins everywhere. Gil

70

chuckled. "It's a tough country, mister," he said under his breath. "You've got to be taught to take it."

The man got up and dusted himself off. Several of those from across the street moved in toward him. They would bait him, now, with caustic advice. Should the man have a sense of humor, the affair would end with several rounds of drinks at one of the saloons.

If Colin Brewster was among those on the street, Gil hadn't seen him. Some distance beyond the Toltec Saloon was a sign which read, DRESSMAKING. Gil headed that way.

Carrie Hawes was a rather plain, dark-haired, middle-aged woman. She told Gil she didn't know what part of the Tetons her father had gone to on his prospecting trip, and she didn't know when he might return. She didn't seem to care, either.

"He's just wasting his time," she said, and there was bitterness in her tone. "He'd be better off if he'd take a job somewhere, but he won't. He'll come back here and sponge off of me as he always does."

There might have been others in town who could give Gil the information he wanted, but he decided against staying around and advertising what was on his mind. For the same reason, he didn't visit Helen Kemp. By dusk he was headed southwest toward Max Sidwell's.

He had no difficulty in locating the Sidwell ranch. The turn-off was well marked. It led him into an area of low, rolling hills and to a sprawling cluster of buildings in a sheltered valley. As he pulled up in the ranch house yard the lights showing through the bunkhouse windows were suddenly extinguished. Gil heard the door open. But no one stepped out.

He dismounted near the corral, tied his horse there, and took another look toward the bunkhouse.

"Who is it?" called a voice. "What do you want?"

Gil remembered how Sam Chenoweth, sitting on his porch, had stiffened and touched his gun when he heard someone riding up in the darkness the night before. Right now, a gun was covering him. He could be sure of it. Here was another sign of the way men lived when they sensed trouble ahead.

"My name's Daly," Gil said. "I want to see Max Sidwell."

"It's all right, Scotty," boomed a voice from the corner of the house. And from that direction, Max Sidwell came striding forward.

"Just playing it safe," he said, grinning. "You know, I really didn't expect to see you again."

Gil chuckled. "That's what Jean Rogers said to me a few hours ago."

"You stopped in Antioch?"

"And suggested she might have a message for you. She didn't send one but her cheeks got sort of pink. Maybe you can read a message in that."

"You catch on pretty quick," Max said. "Come on inside. My mother's gone to bed. Gramps is still up. He's an old war-horse. He'll either like you or he won't, right away. But whichever it is, he'll blister your ears with cussing. He saves up his cuss words all day against the hour when Mom goes to bed. Around Mom, he's meek as a lamb."

72

They entered the house. In a rocking chair, facing the door, sat the thin figure of an old man. The leathery skin of his face was deeply wrinkled, but his eyes seemed sharp. A blanket covered the lower part of his body. Across his lap was a rifle. His gnarled hands gripped it tightly.

"You can put up the rifle, Gramps," Max said lightly. "No trouble yet."

"Maybe I should put it up, maybe I shouldn't," the old man snapped. "Who's he?"

"Well, he used to work on Swallowfork," Max said. "He quit."

"Swallowfork!" The old man followed the word with a chain of epithets. His eyes burned at Gil.

"I've offered him a job, here," Max said when his grandfather ran out of breath.

"A Swallowfork man working on the Double S!" Gramps shouted. "Never!" And he added more profanity.

"I'm not Swallowfork," Gil said mildly. "I don't think I ever was, though I worked there a week. Brewster said I didn't fit in, and I agreed. Another thing — I didn't come here to take a job. At least, not right away."

"Maybe you don't like work," Gramps said. "Most young fellows nowadays are soft. In my time there had to be iron in a man's guts."

It took several minutes to calm the old man down, and even then he wouldn't let Max take his rifle.

Gil pulled off his hat. He offered only a brief explanation for the bandage on his head, saying he thought it was a going-away present from Frank Mills.

"I heard a Swallowfork account of what happened," Max said. "The story is that you jumped Colin Brewster and he mopped up the yard with you."

"The fight didn't last that long," Gil said.

"And what now? That offer of a job still stands."

"And I might want it," Gil said. "Later."

"How much later?"

"After I've found Pete Enders and talked to him."

Max Sidwell rolled a cigaret, stared at it thoughtfully, and then lit it. "Suppose I make a wild guess," he said slowly. "You asked me about Enders back in Antioch. At the same time you asked me if I knew a man named Ed Farley. I said I didn't. Since then I've learned that Farley is the name of the rustler killed on the Swallowfork. And I've learned something else. When old Pete Enders headed into the Toltecs a few months ago, Ed Farley was with him. Logan told me that. So it adds up like this. Farley wasn't a rustler. If he wasn't a rustler, why was he killed?"

"He admitted he was a rustler," Gil said bleakly.

"That's the Swallowfork story."

"Mine too. He admitted he was a rustler, but he admitted it with a rope around his neck and with death staring him in the face. He admitted it on the promise of life, if he talked."

Max whistled. He stared at Gil wide-eyed.

"Brewster was asking who hired him," Gil continued. "He was insisting on one of two names, yours or Logan's. Ed Farley said Logan had hired him. And then, as deliberately as if it had been planned, Frank

Mills slapped the horse Farley was sitting on. The horse jumped out from under him —"

"You mean Farley was lynched? The story I got is that he was shot when he tried to get away."

"He was dangling from the end of a rope, choking to death when Tom Ash put two bullets into his body."

Again Max whistled. He ran his fingers through his hair. He started pacing the room. Gramps was muttering under his breath, cursing Swallowfork. He still gripped his rifle with both hands.

"Gil," Max said abruptly. "Gil, I want you to tell the sheriff what you've just told me. Will you?"

"When I get back."

"Back from where."

"I told you where. I want to find Pete Enders."

"But why? That's the sheriff's job."

"I'm making it mine."

"To get even with Swallowfork? You can even the score a lot quicker and safer just by talking to the sheriff."

Gil shook his head. He wasn't thinking of getting even with Swallowfork. He was thinking of how long it took a man to save up money at cowhand's wages. He was thinking of Ed Farley's ore samples and of the mysterious death of Bill Kemp. He stared at Gramps, conscious of the sharp and penetrating look in the old man's eyes. A scowl settled on his face.

"I'll do this my way," he said stubbornly.

Max Sidwell rode with him that same night to Howard Logan's. And Logan, who had talked with Farley and Pete Enders before they headed into the

Toltecs, gave him the best directions he could, as well as a supply of food. Logan was a thin, round-shouldered man with a drooping mustache. He had a clipped and nervous manner of speech. And he was bitter toward Swallowfork.

Against Logan's advice, and Max Sidwell's, Gil rode on. Dawn found him well into the foothill country and by mid-afternoon he had reached the canyon through which came the water of Squaw Creek. It was up this canyon and beyond the headwaters of Squaw Creek, that Pete Enders and Ed Farley had planned to make their summer camp. From there, they would probe out in several directions. Or at least, such had been their announced intention.

Gil rested for a time, then rode into the canyon. He camped that night in a clearing on the side of the stream, sleeping until dawn; then once more was on his way. But, swerving at one point to cross the stream, he reined up. There, on the sandy bank, he saw the clear hoofprints of a horse which had crossed this way ahead of him. And not too far ahead of him. Perhaps only a few hours.

Excitement pounded through his body. No stray rider would have turned this way. The prints hadn't come there through accident. Someone else had ridden up the canyon ahead of him, and for only one purpose. To see Pete Enders.

Gil didn't push his horse after that. He kept stopping every few minutes to listen. Noon came, mid-afternoon. The canyon suddenly widened, its floor climbing to an almost level plateau. The stream Gil had been following was now only a trickle of water. It curved toward the left wall of the canyon. Over there, somewhere, he should find old Pete's camp. Gil reined up once more. He listened but could hear no sounds from the man ahead. After a moment he swung to the ground and tied his horse to a nearby tree. He moved forward, then, on foot, as silently as he could.

He found the old prospector's camp just after the sun had dropped from sight. It snuggled against a wall of over-hanging rock. To one side was a crude, lean-to shelter. Near it, lay a motionless figure. It was Gil's first thought that old Pete was resting and he wondered about the other man, the man who had come here ahead of him. Then he caught his breath, stiffened, and jerked around, his hand dropping to his gun. Back through the trees he heard the sound of hoofbeats racing away. The sound quickly faded. Whoever had come here ahead of him, had finished his job, returned to his horse, and was now moving down the canyon.

Gil hurried on, then, toward the camp. But the old prospector didn't sit up as he approached. Old Pete Enders would never sit up again. His head was crushed. Around it, in the sand, there spread a darkening stain of blood.

CHAPTER
SEVEN

It was growing dark. The shadows in the canyon were thickening. In another hour they would stretch from wall to wall. For a time, until the moon was up, the man who had left here wouldn't be able to travel very fast, and that was something to think about. There was a good chance that if Gil followed the man, the killer would hear him, and wait to see who was coming. There was a good chance he would run into an ambush.

And there was something else to think about. The man who had killed old Pete Enders, fleeing down canyon, would pass close to where Gil had left his horse. He might see his horse and wait. Or he might turn back.

Gil rolled a cigaret. He had long, strong fingers, usually steady fingers. But they weren't steady tonight. He got the cigaret going, then after several deep puffs he knelt down at the prospector's side. The old man's skin was still warm. He hadn't been dead very long.

If I had only hurried, this wouldn't have happened, Gil told himself. If I had only come a little faster . . .

But there was nothing to be gained through such regrets. He hadn't hurried. He had got here too late.

Still kneeling at the old man's side, he tried to reconstruct what had happened. The killer had reached the camp and found Pete Enders ready to prepare his evening meal. The fire for cooking it was already laid. There had been some talk. And then, after the man learned what he wanted to know, a sudden blow ended the prospector's life.

Gil stood up. He finished his cigaret, dropped it and stamped on it. The shadows were much heavier now. Darkness was lifting up from the floor of the canyon toward the deepening gray of the sky. On the possibility that the killer might have found his horse and turned back, Gil moved over to the shelter Pete Enders had built and stepped inside. And there, seated on the hard packed earth, he waited. An hour passed, another and another. A half moon came climbing into the sky, its pale radiance thinning the shadows. The night grew colder. Gil found a blanket and drew it around his shoulders. There were no strange sounds from the darkness. The man's probably gone, he told himself. I'm a fool to worry about him. But he wasn't sure the man had gone.

But, shortly after dawn, he found his horse still tied where he had left it, and not so far away the trail of the killer, heading down the canyon. He followed that trail for a mile, then grinned wryly and turned back. He had spent an uneasy and apprehensive night for nothing. But that was part of the game, a desperate game — for in Gil's mind there was no question but that the man who had killed Pete Enders, also was the man who had called Bill Kemp outside his home and shot him. Such a man wouldn't hesitate to kill again.

Back at the prospector's camp, Gil Daly took the time to build a rock cairn over old Pete's body. The killer probably had figured that wild animals would soon destroy the evidences of murder, but that couldn't happen now. The pile of rocks would keep animals away.

It was Brewster, Gil thought. It couldn't have been anyone else.

He hunkered down near the cairn of rocks and reviewed in his mind the pattern of what had happened. The Swallowfork riders had captured a man they thought was a rustler. In that belief, the man had been killed. To support this action, Brewster had taken with him to Antioch a sack of ore samples belonging to the rustler, positive that they weren't ore samples. But Kemp, who made the assay, had looked excited as he stepped from his office after Brewster left, and had hurried after Brewster to report his findings. Old Pete had finally made a strike. Brewster, naturally, had asked Kemp to keep quiet, then had made sure Kemp would by shooting him. The next step was to make sure of the location of the strike and then do away with old Pete Enders. This had been accomplished last night. The secret of the location of the gold strike was now Brewster's. He would hold it just as he held the best land in the Rhymer River valley and as he held the river's water.

But it won't work out that way, Gil thought.

80

He had come here to talk to Enders, himself. He had come to stake a claim in what would surely be a worthwhile spot, close to the strike Enders had made. In such a move he had seen a short cut to the future, a quicker way to get his hands on money than working for a monthly wage. The way was still there. He didn't know anything about ore, about where to mark out his claim. But the secret wasn't lost. Brewster held it. He could deal direct with Brewster. He got to his feet, took another look around the camp, and then walked to where his horse was tied. A few minutes later he was riding down the canyon.

Dan Brewster had his noonday meal at Swallowfork with Tom Ash, Hank Morse, and Jim Oldring, and afterward went with Ash to check the barn roof. Several places needed repairs, having been too long neglected. The next few days might be the time to do some work around the ranch. It would keep the men handy for the word he expected from Frank Mills.

Brewster squinted up at the barn roof and at the streaks of sunlight showing through it. He said, "Tom, how are you as a carpenter?"

"I reckon I could do the mending," Ash answered.

"Tomorrow, then," Brewster said. "I'm going to have some of the other men strengthen the corral. We should probably enlarge the root cellar, too. Get things in shape for winter."

Ash pushed back his hat. "Have you sold some cattle to someone, Dan?" he asked bluntly.

"No," Dan Brewster said. "Why?"

"I was down toward Squaw Creek yesterday. Hondo and Lou Crowell were pushing a herd together."

Brewster gave the man a quick hard look. "And why shouldn't they?"

"I was just curious," Ash said. "I'm still curious. Why should Hondo and Crowell be pushing up a herd if you haven't sold any cattle?"

Brewster's edgy anger, always just under the surface, pushed into his voice. "Are you running this place, Tom Ash, or am I?"

"You're running it," Ash said mildly.

"Then let me."

Tom Ash shrugged. "A man still can be curious," he said.

Brewster pulled off his hat. He smoothed his hand over his bald head. He started at Ash, scowling and remembering that in point of years of service, Ash had been here longer than any other man working for him. Perhaps for that reason alone, Ash had a right to be curious. And another thing was driving at Brewster now. The need to justify what he was doing, to lay it on the line for another man's approval. He was being whipsawed by the men who hemmed in Swallowfork. They would be "proving," pretty soon, that the rustler Swallowfork had caught the other day, hadn't been a rustler and that the Swallowfork hadn't been losing cattle. They would lie him into a corner if he gave them a chance.

"Let's put it this way," he said slowly. "I'm tired of losing cattle. I'm tired of being played a sucker. Logan ran off fifty head of our cattle the other day. We caught

82

one of the men working for him but by the time we got the sheriff out here the trail was cold. Cold enough so he wasn't able to see it. Those cattle you saw being rounded up are going to be drifted close to Logan's range, and we're going to watch them. When Logan grabs them — and he will — we're going after him. We're going to nail him for the crook he is."

"What if he doesn't grab them?"

"He will."

"Or maybe we'll push them across his line? Is that it?"

"We won't have to. But if we did, it would be no more than right."

Tom Ash shook his head. He studied Brewster, then looked away. He said, "Dan, I've worked here a long time, maybe too long a time. I've never wondered about what the country was like, over the hills. That is, until lately. Lately I've been wondering."

Dan Brewster's lips tightened. "Maybe you'd better go and see."

Ash sighed, then nodded. "Yes, maybe I should."

They were in the barn. It was hot in the barn. Brewster again mopped his hand over his head, brushing off the perspiration. He told himself, "I ought to say something. This could be patched up. It isn't right for Tom Ash to leave Swallowfork." But he remained silent. Ash really didn't fit in with Swallowfork any more. He could take it when the going was easy, but when it got rough his soft spot showed up. It would be better for Ash and better for Swallowfork to call it quits right now.

"I reckon I'll pack my stuff, Dan," Ash said after a moment of silence.

Brewster left the barn abruptly. He felt almost sad, almost guilty.

But back in the ranch house, figuring out how much money Ash had coming to him, he let anger hit him again. What right had Tom Ash to walk out like this? He was already short handed. The departure of Tom Ash would make the situation worse, and at a time when he needed every available man. He was storming back and forth across the room when Colin came in.

"What's the matter with you?" Colin asked.

Brewster's words were explosive. "I've just had a run-in with Tom Ash. What's wrong with the way I run Swallowfork?"

"Plenty," Colin said. "Several men need firing. Tom Ash is one of them. He's a lily-livered old man."

"What makes you say that?"

Colin tossed his hat toward the hall tree. It caught on one of the hooks and hung there, swaying back and forth. A grin crossed the young man's face. He said. "Made it." And then, "What's biting Tom Ash?"

Colin apparently was in one of his rare good moods, ready and willing to talk, with no chip on his shoulder. Brewster sensed that, warming immediately toward his son. There were many things he would like to talk over with Colin, many confidences he would like to exchange, but it wasn't often they could talk with each other. They seemed to clash over almost everything. Colin had a temper as quick as his, or quicker. Colin would seldom listen to what he had to say, and would never listen if his words came in the nature of advice.

"Well, are you going to tell me?" Colin was asking.

"Why not?" said Brewster. "Some day, the Swallowfork will be yours. Some day its problems will be yours."

"When that happens, there'll be a few changes made."

Brewster sighed. "It'll be up to you."

"I wish it was up to me now. At least, you could get rid of Frank Mills. Why shouldn't I be foreman?"

They were getting on dangerous ground. They had been over all this before, had wrangled about it. Brewster quickly changed the subject. "Let me tell you about Tom Ash," he suggested. "He rode south the other day and saw Hondo and Lou Crowell pushing up a herd. He wanted to know why. When I told him, he didn't like what I said."

Colin was scowling. He stood with his feet far apart, his hands on his hips, his head pushed forward. Short, stocky, and with a powerful body, he was a match for anyone on the ranch. And ready for a fight, any time. "Well, why are they pushing up a herd?" he demanded.

"They're going to shove some cattle close to Logan's range," Brewster said, and he was careful not to mention that this had been Frank Mill's idea. "Logan will grab them. He won't be able to help it. We'll be watching. When Logan makes his grab, we ride after him. The men who have been bleeding Swallowfork need a lesson. They're going to get it."

A slow grin broke across Colin's face. "Now, you're talking," he agreed. "I've been waiting to hear something like this. If Ash doesn't like it, let him go. He wouldn't be much help to us anyhow."

"He's going," Brewster said. "He's packing his stuff. But with Ash gone we'll be short handed."

Colin bit his lips, glowering thoughtfully. "Supposing Ash should talk? Supposing Logan got word of what we're planning?"

"I don't think Ash will talk."

"If I were running things, I'd make sure he didn't," Colin snapped. He crossed to the halltree and got his hat.

"Where are you going?" Brewster asked.

"Out."

The word was harsh and there was a challenge in it. A challenge to Brewster's right to question him. A moment before they had been in accord but it had been a brief accord. Brewster put his finger on what had gone wrong. Colin didn't like it that he was being easy on Tom Ash. There was a bitter and ruthless drive in Colin which sometimes frightened him, and here was an example of it.

"Tom Ash has been with Swallowfork a long time," he said slowly. "You've got to remember a thing like that, Colin."

"Like hell I do," Colin said, and left his father standing alone in the room.

Tom Ash finished his packing. It hadn't taken long, and that rather amazed him. It seemed strange that a man could live at a place half of his adult life, and in the space of a few minutes and one bag, store away all he wanted to carry with him. And it was strange to be leaving on such scant notice.

He sat on the edge of his bunk, rolled a cigaret, lit it, and stared scowling at the floor, realizing that his decision hadn't been so sudden after all. For a year it had been in his mind. For more than a year. Swallowfork had changed. In the old days when Mrs. Brewster had been alive and Colin was growing up, there hadn't been a better place to work anywhere. In the old days there hadn't been trouble over water rights, and the men on the bordering ranches had been neighbors. In the old days, a man hadn't had to wear a gun.

Ash had spent considerable time in trying to analyze and understand the change which had come over the basin. He attributed it, chiefly, to four things. One was, aside from Swallowfork, an external reason, and perhaps important but not all important. The recent years had been hard. There had been a long drought and cattle prices, sagging several years ago, hadn't yet picked up though the market was some better. To combat the drought and protect Swallowfork cattle, Brewster had dammed the Rhymer River and several other streams crossing the basin. The courts had made him blow up the dams but Brewster still controlled the water through temporary dams which would divert the streams to flood his meadows. And the men on the ranches around Swallowfork, and beyond, knew what he was doing. It didn't make them love Dan Brewster.

But three other factors had contributed to the change in Swallowfork. Dan Brewster had changed. Colin had grown up. And a new crew — new excepting for him and Frank Mills — had, in the past few years, replaced the men who'd worked here in the old days. The core of the trouble was here. Ash was satisfied of that. The core of the conflict was in Brewster himself, and in his relationship to his son, and the surly tempers of the present Swallowfork crew.

Ash finished his cigaret, pinched out the fire and stood up. He shouldered his war-bag, left the bunkhouse, and crossed to where his horse was tied. As he was fixing the war-bag over the blanket roll, behind the saddle, he noticed three men riding off to the north — Colin, Hank Morse, and Jim Oldring — but it didn't even occur to him to wonder where they were going.

He heard footsteps approaching from the ranch house, turned, and saw Dan Brewster.

"Here's your money," Brewster said, his voice gruff. "I added a bonus."

"You didn't have to," Tom Ash said.

He took the money Brewster was holding out to him. He shoved it into his pocket without counting it. He untied his horse and climbed into the saddle.

"Where are you riding," Brewster added.

"North," Ash said. "Over the hills."

Brewster nodded. His frown vanished. He said, "Good luck, Tom," and he sounded as though he meant it.

"Thanks, Dan," said Tom Ash.

He lifted his reins, wheeled his horse away toward the road. His eyes were a little misty and he felt choked up. Before he had gone very far he looked back. He could see Dan still in the yard, watching him. He looked toward the porch, remembering how Mrs. Brewster used to come out and wave to him sometimes, Colin with her. Always with her, never with his father. It had hit Colin terribly hard when his mother died.

Tom Ash didn't hurry. He had no destination in mind. He would turn north when he came to the main road. There was no reason to go to Antioch, no one he had to say good-by to. He could stop in at Charlie Weseloh's for supper. He and Charlie got along in spite of recent troubles in the basin.

He came to the main road, crossed the Rhymer River bridge and took the climb up the bluff above Four Mile Creek. Once there, he reined up. Someone was riding down the road, toward him. In a moment he recognized Myra Chenoweth. He moved on, reining up again as he met her.

"Hello, Myra," he said. "You're not going to town this late, are you?"

"It can't be helped," the girl told him. "Dad has an important letter to get off. I'll stay overnight with Jean Rogers. But where are you heading, Tom?"

"North," said Tom. "Just north."

"You're not leaving?"

"I'm afraid I am."

"After all the years you've been at Swallowfork?"

"Too many years." Tom Ash grinned ruefully. "I've been wondering what's over the hills. If I put it off too long, I'll be too old to ever find out."

"Dad will be sorry you're leaving Swallowfork," said Myra Chenoweth. "He'll be sorry he didn't get to tell you good-by."

Tom Ash nodded, realizing that was probably true. It occurred to him that there probably were others who would be sorry he was gone. He still had a few friends in the basin. Old friends.

"I may come back some day," he said slowly. "Tell your father good-by for me, and best of luck to you, Myra. When you pick a man, pick a good one."

"How can I, when you're leaving the basin?" Myra said, laughing.

Tom Ash joined in her laughter, for a moment feeling young again and aware of the warmth of this girl's dark eyes and of her supple, slender figure. The man who won her, he knew, would be mighty lucky. There was strength as well as beauty in Myra Chenoweth. And rare judgment. It hadn't taken her long to discourage Colin Brewster.

They talked for a moment longer, then Tom Ash rode on and Myra continued down the road. But Ash had traveled only a few hundred yards when he heard sounds behind him. He twisted in the saddle and looked back. Three mounted men had stopped Myra Chenoweth at the point where the road dropped down the Rhymer River bridge, and as Ash looked back, one of the men left the group and came galloping toward him. Almost immediately, Ash recognized the man as Colin Brewster.

A sudden apprehension came over him. His fingers touched his holstered gun, then fell away. He reined up. Across his mind flashed a memory from the past, a memory of Colin as a boy of thirteen or fourteen, screaming at him and calling him a liar in a charge so absolutely false that even Dan Brewster had had to side against his son. From that day on, Colin had disliked him, though in Dan Brewster's presence he usually hid his feelings.

Tom Ash tensed. The apprehension he had felt a moment before was stronger. Beyond the approaching Colin he could see two men, still with Myra Chenoweth. One had grabbed the reins of her horse as though to keep her from riding on. But why? Why had Myra been stopped and why was Colin riding after him?

Colin reached him and pulled up, hauling back on the reins of his horse with an almost vicious pull. A gun was in Colin's other hand, a gun leveled straight at him, and the young man's dark eyes were glistening with anger.

"What did you tell her?" Colin shouted at him. "Out with it, Ash. How much of the story did you spill?"

"What story?" Tom Ash asked, confused.

"About what we're going to do to Logan. How much did you tell her?"

"Why, I didn't tell her anything. I met her on the road. We stopped and said hello. That was all."

"You're lying!"

The words were shouted. Colin's face was flushed, his lips drawn tight across his teeth. He was leaning forward in the saddle.

"You're lying," he repeated. "You told her the whole story. You asked her to get word to Logan. You've never stood back of Swallowfork, never thought Swallowfork was right. You left to sell us out. But it won't work, Ash."

A glimmer of understanding came to Tom Ash. This wasn't a grown man facing him. Colin Brewster, in a man's image, was still a little boy, shouting out his rage, screaming his anger. And you couldn't reason with a little boy. His mind wasn't open to reason.

"Listen," said Ash. "I didn't —"

"No, you listen," Colin said. "Listen to this —"

Ash heard the roar of a gun. He felt a blow in the chest. He stared wide-eyed at Colin Brewster and at the gun in Colin's hand. A little smoke drifted from the muzzle of the gun. It seemed to spread out, casting a film between them. Dull pain lifted up to Ash's throat. The image of Colin faded, disappeared. Why, I've been shot, Ash thought. That was what I heard. A shot. But even Colin . . .

The thought ran out, unfinished. Ash twisted in the saddle and spilled to the road. But he didn't know it. He would never see the country which lay beyond the hills, but he didn't know that, either.

CHAPTER
EIGHT

Myra Chenoweth sat rigidly on the back of her horse. She hadn't been frightened when Colin and his two companions stopped her. She hadn't been frightened at their questions, only indignant. But she was frightened now. Suddenly and terribly frightened. She saw, up the road, the body of Tom Ash reel from the saddle. She saw his horse dance away, saw Colin ride after it and catch it. She shook her head, not wanting to believe what her mind told her was true, that Tom Ash was dead.

"I figured Colin would do it," said the man holding the bridle of her horse.

"Yep, I did too," said the other man. "He's a fellow to watch, even when he's on your side."

Myra glanced at the two men. She knew them by sight as Swallowfork riders. She thought one was named Hank Morse, but she wasn't sure. They weren't old men but their faces were old, tight-lined, unsmiling. Their eyes were sharp, nervous.

It didn't occur to Myra to wonder what they meant to do with her. She was too stunned at what had happened, at the suddeness of it. She couldn't understand the meaning of it. When the three men had stopped her and asked what Tom Ash had told her, she had said only that he'd told her good-by. Colin, unreasonably, had refused to believe her. "He told you about Logan," Colin shouted at her. "You might as well admit it. He spilled the whole story."

But Tom Ash hadn't told her a thing about Logan.

Myra looked up the road again. Colin had caught Tom Ash's horse and now seemed to be tying the old man's body across it. He was having trouble. The horse was skittish.

"I wish he'd hurry," Hank Morse said.

"No one's gonna come along," said the other man. "What's the rush?"

No one was going to come along. Those words found an echo in Myra's thoughts. The body of Tom Ash would be carried away and no one would know what had happened here on the road above Four Mile Creek. No one but those who had witnessed it.

Colin came back toward them, leading Ash's horse, the old man's body tied across the saddle. When he pulled up, he stared at them almost defiantly, but with a different look in his eyes. A defensive look. "Well, what else could I do?" he said sharply. "Ash went for his gun. He asked for it."

"Sure he did," Hank Morse said. "Forget it."

The other man nodded. Myra said nothing.

"What about the girl?" Morse asked.

"We'll take her with us to Swallowfork," Colin said. "She can visit us a few days. The old man will like that, anyhow."

94

Myra still said nothing, but she made herself a promise. Taking her to Swallowfork wouldn't silence her. People would still hear about what had happened on the road above Four Mile Creek.

Colin looked at the body of Tom Ash, then at Myra, and suddenly he laughed. It was a short laugh. It was high and shrill and sounded unreal. Colin had laughed that way at the sight of Ed Farley's body dangling at the end of a rope.

They rode down the hill, across the Rhymer River bridge, and took the road toward Swallowfork, Hank Morse in front, leading Myra's horse by its bridle. Behind them, Jim Oldring, Colin, and another led horse with the stiffening body of Tom Ash across the saddle. The warmth of the day was passing. Far to the west, the sun was dropping down toward the blue peaks of the Rincons. In two hours it would be dusk. By the time they got to the ranch night would have come.

Myra Chenoweth sat erect in the saddle, looking neither right nor left. Hank Morse had spoken to her several times but she hadn't answered him, and given no indication she had heard him. Underneath the calm she was showing, she was still frightened, but another emotion was stirring through her fear. The beginning of anger. She could feel it pounding at her, could feel it tightening her muscles. These men could take her to Swallowfork but they couldn't hold her there. Not unless she was watched every minute, watched constantly.

She remembered the letter she had to mail. She had told Tom Ash it was an important letter. Actually, it wasn't. Actually, it had only been an excuse to go to town where she meant to spend the night with Jean Rogers. Her father, in town the day before, had heard from Jean that Gil Daly had been in Antioch, and this had made Myra curious. She had assumed Gil was riding on north, that after his trouble with Swallowfork he was getting out of the country. Her father hadn't questioned Jean about the young man, but Myra had meant to. She had offered Gil a job on the ranch but he had turned it down, reminding her caustically that Swallowfork didn't want him around. Why, then, had he gone to Antioch?

But this problem, now, was of minor importance. Myra stared straight ahead, her face stony. Behind her she could hear the occasional sound of Colin's voice as he spoke to Jim Oldring, and could hear Oldring's reply. Once, Howard Logan's name was mentioned, and this reminded her that it was what Ash was supposed to have told her about Logan which had started all this trouble. She tried to listen to what Colin and Oldring were saying about Logan, but what she heard didn't make much sense.

"When he grabs them, we go after him," Colin said. "That's all there is to it."

"What about the law?" Oldring asked.

"The law will have to back us up, if that's important."

Their voices became indistinguishable as they dropped farther behind. Myra puzzled over what they had said.

96

It was dark by the time they reached the ranch house and pulled up in the yard. Colin swung to the ground. He handed the reins of Ash's horse to Jim Oldring and said, "I'll see the old man. Put the body in the barn, unsaddle his horse and turn it into the corral."

Oldring nodded.

"And you wait here with our guest," Colin said to Hank Morse, chuckling. "The old man's going to like part of what we brought back."

Myra's lips tightened. She watched Colin move up to the ranch house, pull open the door and step inside.

Gil Daly had his noonday meal while still in the canyon. He rode on, then, and breaking out of the canyon, followed the trail of Pete Ender's slayer. It led almost due east, along Squaw Creek, twisting finally out of the foothills and into the basin of the Swallowfork. Half an hour later, topping a low rise, Gil saw a herd of several hundred cattle below. Three men were pushing them south. He reined up quickly and turned back. Once out of sight he dismounted, ground-hitched his horse, and climbed the hill on foot.

The three men driving the herd apparently hadn't seen him, or at least hadn't turned his way. He thought he recognized the three as Hondo, Lou Crowell and Frank Mills. Mills, he was sure of. The chunky figure of the Swallowfork foreman was easily distinguishable.

This was still hilly country, and below Squaw Creek, toward which the herd was moving, there seemed to be more hills. Why these men were driving the cattle in that direction, Gil couldn't understand. The Swallowfork range extended only a few miles below Squaw Creek.

Maybe Brewster's going to get another report on rustling, Gil thought. Maybe Hondo, Crowell and Mills are the rustlers, with a little help from someone to the south.

He considered such a possibility for a time, realizing that it wasn't at all improbable. Men on other large ranches had helped themselves to their employers' cattle. It wasn't a thing unheard of.

Yet one fact didn't fit in. The man whose trail he had followed from Enders' camp had come this way, and would have seen this herd and the men driving it south. In his own mind, Gil had decided it was Brewster who had been at Enders' camp. Brewster then, would have seen what was happening, and would have done something about it. Or would he? Even Dan Brewster might hesitate about jumping three men, alone.

Gil watched the herd for a time, then backed down the hill and walked to where he had left his horse. He swung into the saddle and headed north. This rustling was no concern of his. The problems of the Swallowfork basin and of the ranchers in the northern Rhymer River valley were problems other people could deal with. His interest lay in what old Pete Enders might have said to Dan Brewster about the location of a mining claim.

He reached the Rhymer River at dusk, stopped for a hurried evening meal which he ate cold from the supplies he was carrying, and then rode on, circling a little to the west. He knew this part of the country, was again on familiar ground. Three hours later he skirted a wooded area which extended down a broad valley and at its far edge pulled up. Just ahead of him, now, were the ranch buildings of the Swallowfork. The main ranch house and its several cabins, one of which was used by Frank Mills and his wife. The bunkhouse, the barn, the sheds. Lamp light showed around the curtained windows of the ranch house, indicating that Dan Brewster hadn't yet gone to bed. And there was a good chance, Gil knew, of finding Brewster alone. Colin spent most of his nights in town, or with the men in the bunkhouse. He didn't enjoy his father's company. And it wasn't often that Brewster invited his men to the house.

Gil swung to the ground. He tied his horse to one of the trees and moved forward, passing the barn, crossing the yard, and climbing the porch steps. It was only a step to the door. Gil took it. He reached for his holstered gun, pulled it free, then felt with his left hand for the doorknob. A smile tugged at his lips. The door was never locked, but maybe, after tonight, it would be. He turned the knob and pushed. The door opened easily.

As long as he lived Gil would never forget the shock of what he saw when the door opened and when he looked into the lighted front room of the ranch house. Facing him, seated in a rocker, her hands in her lap, was Myra Chenoweth. Nothing else, no scene of violence would have been as startling as this, for Myra Chenoweth, as Gil had thought of her, didn't belong here. Myra was at another point of the compass from

Swallowfork and Dan Brewster. Yet here she was, in a rocking chair in Brewster's parlor, staring straight at him.

There was immediate recognition in the girl's eyes. She stopped rocking the chair. Gil heard the catch of her breath.

"Colin?" said Dan Brewster. "Colin, come on in. I want to talk to you again, anyhow."

Dan Brewster sat at the table, his back to the door, an open ledger in front of him. He turned toward Gil as he spoke. Turned, and saw who was there, and pushed back his chair and came to his feet. His hand dropped toward his hip but he wasn't wearing his gun. He had unbuckled his gun belt earlier, and had hung it on a nail near the fireplace. His eyes flicked that way, then came back to Gil. Sharp eyes, dark, hard, and holding a threat of violence.

Gil stepped into the room. He kicked the door shut and stood against it, the gun in his hand covering Brewster. He felt a little exicted. He wasn't used to a thing like this and the presence of Myra Chenoweth made him uneasy. But Brewster could understand a gun. Even Myra could understand a gun.

"I didn't know you had company," he said slowly. "Maybe I should have knocked."

There was direct accusation in his voice and in his words. Color flamed in Myra's face. She came quickly to her feet.

"Ask him why I'm here!" she cried. "Ask him what happened to Tom Ash! Ask him what the Swallowfork plans to do to Howard Logan!"

Here were questions which struck no answering chord in Gil's mind. Here was an indication of developments of which he didn't know. But one thing was abruptly clear. He could read it in the almost hysterical note of Myra's voice as well as in what she had said. The girl wasn't here because she wanted to be. She wasn't here of her own free will. Gil was aware of an immediate lift. What he had come here to say to Brewster could go for a while. He was to have a chance to repay Myra Chenoweth for the help she had given him.

"How about it, Brewster?" he asked bluntly.

The older man shook his head. "I'll answer to you for nothing I do. I fired you from Swallowfork. If you're smart you'll back out that door and leave."

"Suppose we both back out the door and leave, Myra and I."

"You won't get far."

Gil glanced at the girl. "How about it, Myra?"

She came toward him immediately. "They brought me here," she said swiftly, her words almost running together. "I met Tom Ash on the road and talked to him for a moment. I saw him killed. They thought he had told me what they are planning to do to Howard Logan, so they brought me here."

"Tom Ash is dead?" Gil said.

"He was shot by Colin. He was leaving the country. He hadn't told me a thing, but since then I've heard enough to know what they plan on doing."

Gil nodded his head but he was hardly listening to the girl's words. He was remembering Tom Ash, who had shot the strangling rustler, bringing a swift end to the man's suffering. Tom Ash, who in the yard in front of the corral in Antioch had warned him to make a break for it. Tom Ash, whose face would never take a burn and whose lips were always cracked and sore. He hadn't known Tom Ash very well, hadn't known him much better than the other men on Swallowfork; but during the week he had been here it had usually been Tom Ash who fell in beside him on a ride, or who paired off with him on a job.

He glanced at Myra. A few minutes before, just after he came in, she had sounded almost hysterical. She was still upset, but he could understand that. Some girls, facing the uncertainties she must have faced during the evening, would have been in a state of collapse.

"What's the plan about Logan?" he asked.

"They've pushed a herd up close to the north border of Logan's range," Myra answered. "They're going to drive it south, but claim that Logan did it. They're going to use that as an excuse for a raid on Logan's. As they were bringing me here I heard Colin say they were ready to go ahead tomorrow night."

Brewster took a step forward, anger showing in his face. "There's not a word of truth in that, Myra. I told you before that you misunderstood what you heard Colin say. When he comes back from wherever he's gone, he'll tell you so himself."

"You are pushing up a herd, south of here," Gil said. "I saw them."

"We moved some cattle to one of our south pastures," Brewster said. "What's so wrong about that?"

"I know what I heard," Myra said stubbornly. "I know what you're planning. I didn't misunderstand anything. If what you claim is true, why did you keep me here, a prisoner?"

Brewster shook his head. "That's another thing you're wrong about. You came here of your own free will. You came with a wild story of how Tom Ash was killed, and of what I was planning to do to Logan. I've been trying to convince you how mistaken you were. As for being a prisoner, you can leave here any time you wish."

Myra swung to face Gil, her eyes wide with shock. "He's lying, Gil. He's lying. Every word he's said is a lie."

Gil chuckled. "Sure, he's lying. Covering up for Colin. And since you learned what he was planning for Logan he didn't dare let you go. But I think he will, now. See if you can find a rope on the back porch."

The girl hurried from the room.

Brewster's scowl deepened. He stole another glance at his holstered gun near the fireplace. It was too far away to reach. He smoothed his hand over his shiny, bald head, then gave a tug at his beard. It was a General Grant beard, neatly trimmed, and showing only a few streaks of gray. "You'll be sorry for this," he muttered heavily. "As long as you live you'll be sorry for it."

"But I may not live long," Gil said, grinning.

"You won't," Brewster promised.

Myra returned to the room with a coil of rope. She gave it to Gil and took his gun, covering Brewster with it. She held the gun as though she knew how to use it.

It took only a few minutes to bind and gag the Swallowfork owner. Gil worked swiftly, his mind active. He and Myra would get away from here. It had been his first thought that they would go together, but he wondered, now, if some other plan wouldn't be better. The minute they left here, Brewster might decide to push ahead with his raid on Logan, acting before Myra could arouse anyone to stand in his way. In fact, Brewster would have to act in a hurry, or give up the scheme altogether. And Brewster wasn't a man who liked to back down.

Gil finished his work with the rope, then took the gun from Myra's hand. "Ready?" he asked her. And he smiled, hoping to ease the tension he knew she was feeling.

"I was never more ready in my life," said Myra Chenoweth. A smile pulled at her lips. Her fingers found his hand and squeezed it, and she added, "Thanks, Gil. If you hadn't shown up when you did —"

Gil lowered his voice. "I've been thinking about this plan of Brewster's. There's a chance he might head for Logan's tonight, soon as we get away from here. One of us ought to ride to town and tell the sheriff what to expect. You do that. I'll warn Logan."

Myra nodded.

"There are several horses tied to the corral fence," Gil continued. "Take one. Lead him off a ways, then burn up the road to town. My horse is tied at the edge of the grove beyond the barn. I'll head for Logan's."

Again the girl nodded. They moved through the darkened kitchen and across a narrow back porch. Gil reached for Myra's hand and held it a moment, tightly.

"Take it slow and easy before you get away from here," he whispered.

"Take it slow and easy yourself," she whispered back.

She turned toward the corner of the house and stood there for a moment, a blurred, shadowy figure, scarcely visible in the darkness. Then, in another instant, she was gone.

CHAPTER
NINE

Gil turned back into the house. He crossed the front room, hardly glancing at Brewster who was struggling with his bonds, and for a time, then, he stood at the front door, listening. But there were no sounds from the yard to indicate that anyone was aware of Myra's escape. Satisfied, finally, that the girl was safely away, Gil looked around at the owner of Swallowfork.

Brewster had stopped trying to free himself. His eyes, hard and dark, met Gil's without flinching. Muffled sounds came around the gag stuffed into his mouth and tied there.

"You surely hate it when you can't talk, don't you," Gil said, grinning at Brewster.

He moved forward. He stood facing the man, the grin on his lips slowly disappearing. "I came here to tell you something, Brewster," he said slowly. "What I ran into sort of got in the way, but we'll get back to it one of these days because I'm going to be around for quite a while. Yep, quite a while."

Again those muffled sounds came around the gag in Brewster's mouth.

"Here's part of it," Gil said. "Part of what I wanted to tell you. I know about the assay report on the ore samples you took to Bill Kemp. I know why Kemp was killed. I was at the headwaters of Squaw Creek last night when another man was killed. Old Pete Enders. I know why he had to be killed. I know the same secrets you do, Brewster. It's something you can think about. Something you'd better think about mighty hard."

The eyes looking up at him seemed to widen, and there was a puzzled look in them, an uncomprehending look. Again meaningless noises came around the gag in Brewster's mouth.

"Nope, I don't want to hear you now," Gil said. "But maybe the next time we meet —"

He broke off what he was saying. There had been a sound behind him, at the door. He swung around, clawing at his holster. He heard the roar of a gun and felt the scraping pain of a bullet as it scratched the flesh of his shoulder. It was Colin at the door — Colin, who had opened it without knocking, who had seen his father bound in a chair with some man standing over him, and who had fired too hastily.

Gil threw a quick shot at Colin, who was already backing out the door. It was a wasted shot, and he knew it the moment his finger squeezed the trigger. The door slammed shut but from out on the porch he could hear Colin shouting for Slim Gorman and Hank Morse and the others. How many Swallowfork riders were in the bunkhouse, Gil didn't know, but any number was too many. He had overstayed his time with Brewster. He should have left when Myra did. He shouldn't have come back.

There would be no escape through the front door, Gil knew. He turned to the back, pounding through the darkened kitchen and across the porch. As he stepped outside he heard someone running along the side of the house and he swung the other way. A bullet screamed past his head and he heard Gorman shouting, "He's back here, Colin. Back here!"

Another bullet tugged at Gil's flapping coat. He dived to the ground, twisting around as he fell. He looked back, fired at the flash mark of a gun, then rolled quickly away and lay motionless, his eyes probing the shadows. It was dark, but not dark enough. There was a crouching figure on his left, another to his right. The one to his left was Gorman and he heard Gorman shouting, "I've winged him, Colin. He's down."

"Then move in and finish him," Colin shouted. "Morse is circling to the north."

Gil pulled in a long, slow breath. He wasn't winged. Not yet. But these men would have him boxed in before long if he didn't get out of here. He could be sure of that. They knew just about where he was. They could close in slowly. After a time, someone would spot his exact position. This would happen more quickly if he risked another shot. The flash of his gun would show where he was lying. He had two choices, neither very good. He could stay here and take it, or he could gamble on a quick break.

He twisted around on the ground. Lying flat on his face, he pulled his body forward, away from the house. He covered maybe a dozen yards this way, then glanced back. He could see neither of the two men between him and the house. Both were probably as flat to the ground as he was. He stared ahead but could see nothing of Morse. He came slowly to his knees, every muscle in his body tensed against the shock of a bullet. His breath was coming faster. A clammy perspiration chilled him.

He straightened up. He started running. Behind him, Colin screamed a hoarse warning. Shots laced through the air. How close any came, Gil didn't know. He saw the lumbering figure of Hank Morse cutting in toward him from the side. Morse was firing wildly. Gil's arm whipped up. He felt the kick of his gun as he squeezed the trigger. He saw Morse stop, rock sideways, and go down.

The grove where he had tied his horse was to the left. Gil swung that way. He tripped over something, sprawled to the ground, got up again and took a quick look over his shoulder. The firing had stopped, but probably only until Colin and Gorman and whoever else was with them could reload their guns. They were still moving after him. He could see the vague outlines of several figures. They were moving after him, but he was close to the grove, now. Close to where he had left his horse. Close to getting away.

He holstered his gun. When he reached his horse he pulled the reins free and swung to the saddle. A moment later he was heading south, in the direction of Howard Logan's. But it was a long time before he could relax. His escape had been by too narrow a margin for any comfort. And there was something else to think about. Tonight, in what he had said to

Brewster, and in what he had done, he had put a price on his own head.

A wry grin twisted his lips. Ride hard, Myra, he said under his breath. Find the sheriff and get him to Logan's. I'm afraid we'll need him.

But Myra wasn't riding toward Antioch. After she left Gil she moved to the front corner of the house and started toward the corral. The horses Gil had mentioned were there, tied to the fence. Myra hurried forward. She reached the place where the horses were tied, then suddenly stiffened and looked back over her shoulder toward the bunkhouse. It's door had opened. Two men had stepped out. One, she recognized as Colin. Who the other man was she didn't know.

Standing close against the corral fence, she waited, almost holding her breath. The two men started toward the horses, then stopped. They were having some kind of argument. She could hear the low murmur of their voices.

"But why not throw in with us, Jim?" Colin was insisting. "What have you got to lose?"

"What have I got to gain, for that matter?" came the answer. "What's a few dollars from the sale of rustled cattle?"

"It'll be more than a few dollars," Colin said. "It could even be enough to get a place of your own."

"You don't make that kind of money from rustled cattle."

"Don't you?" said Colin. "Listen to this . . ."

His voice lowered, grew indistinct. Myra leaned forward. She had forgotten for the moment the necessity of getting away. Here was the hint of something she would never have suspected. She wanted to hear more, wanted to understand, wanted to know what kind of rustling Colin was talking about.

She had no warning that she had been discovered. One moment the two men were whispering together. In another, they had whirled around and were racing toward her. Myra dived for the corral fence. She tried to slip between its rails, but not in time. Colin reached her. He caught her shoulder, his fingers digging sharply into her flesh. He pulled her back and slammed her to the ground, twisting her arm up behind her so tightly that she was afraid it would break. The pain brought a cry to her lips, a cry she couldn't smother.

Colin instantly released the pressure on her arm. He started laughing. He called, "Jim, we've caught us a woman. And I'll bet I know who she is."

He released her completely, rolling her over. Still on his knees, he struck a match, his cupped hands reflecting its light into her face. After a moment he blew the match out and stood up.

"I wonder why the old man let her go," he muttered, and he sounded worried. "Keep her here, Jim, while I ask him."

"Sure, Colin," said the man called Jim. "I'll keep her here."

Myra sat up. Her braids had come loose but she didn't try to twist them back into place. She still felt a little breathless from her struggle with Colin, but she was more worried than hurt. Worried, and disappointed in herself. Right now she should be on her way to Antioch. And she might have made it even if these men had seen her escaping and followed her.

Jim struck a match to light the cigaret he had made, and Myra, looking up, caught a glimpse of his face. A thin face, hard-lined, unshaven. A face with sharp and irregular features. She recognized it immediately. Jim was one of the two men who had been with Colin this afternoon, and who had brought her here. His last name was Oldring.

Two shots from the direction of the house startled her. She looked that way and saw Colin backing out of the door. Then she heard him shouting for Slim Gorman and Hank Morse. The bunkhouse door burst open. Several men came hurrying out. Colin was barking orders from the front of the house.

Jim Oldring dropped down beside her. He put out a restraining hand when she started to get up. "It's a good idea to keep close to the ground at times like this," he said. "We'll get along, sister. We'll sit this one out."

There was a burst of shooting from behind the house. Colin hurried that way. There was more shooting. Jim Oldring's arm was still across Myra's shoulders, and now, suddenly, he pulled her toward him, half over his lap.

"You know," he said thickly, "I don't mind this a bit. In fact, I'm glad Colin left me here with you."

Both his arms closed around her. His face came down hard against hers, the bristle of his beard scratching her cheek. Myra tried to twist away. She got a hand against Oldring's face and pushed. Her fingers slipped up and caught in his hair and her other hand raked at his face while she was still trying to twist away.

She almost made it, but he caught her again as she was pulling free, and threw her back on the ground. Myra twisted toward him, stabbing a blow at his face. She hit at him again but he caught her wrist, and then her other wrist, and held them in a grip she couldn't break. Straddling her body, he got his knees on her arms, pinning them down, but with most of his weight on her stomach.

Myra had at first been too startled to be aware of any fear of this man. Now she was too angry. In spite of the weight of his body and the grinding pressure of his knees, she tried to wrench free. Her breath was coming heavily, but so was Oldring's. Words rumbled from his throat. "What's the matter with you, anyhow? Maybe you think you're too good for a man like me. You've got a few things to learn, sister. No woman's too good for Jim Oldring."

He leaned toward her. As his head came down, Myra jerked her head up. Her forehead broke Oldring's lips against his teeth. He reared back, swearing at her, his knees sliding from her arms. And Myra took full advantage of this lapse. She reached up and caught his hair again, jerking his head sideways, twisting her body. A slamming fist caught her on the side of the head, almost stunning her. The fist slammed at her again, and through a gathering fog she heard Oldring swearing. Then she felt his hands again on her shoulders, pulling her toward him. This time, she didn't have the strength to resist.

But Jim Oldring did not have his way with her.

Another burst of gunfire died beyond the house. Colin's voice cut through the darkness: "Hey, Oldring. Bring the girl inside."

Jim Oldring stood up. He pulled Myra to her feet and watched as she staggered back to the corral fence and leaned there, wiping her hand across her mouth.

"Come on," he said gruffly. "We'll get together again some other time."

He reached out as though to help her walk to the house but Myra slapped his hand away.

"Never touch me again," she said fiercely. "Never touch me again as long as you live."

She pushed past him, starting toward the house, but not sure she could make it that far alone. There was still a ringing sound in her ears and her legs seemed leaden. But the fogginess was gone. A sharp and driving anger was taking its place. A strengthening anger. She lifted her head, squared her shoulders. She reached the porch, climbed the porch steps and moved past Colin who was holding the door open.

"What in the world happened to you?" Colin asked.

"She tried to get away," said Jim Oldring, who had followed her. "She's a regular wildcat."

Colin grunted.

Myra said nothing. She knew she looked terrible. Her hair had come down and was half unbraided. Her clothing was torn. There were bruise marks on her face.

114

"Well, shall I go after him?" Colin was asking his father.

"If you think you can catch him," Brewster said. "And if you can shoot straight when you get him under your gun."

"I can shoot straight enough," Colin snapped. "I didn't have a chance at him outside."

"You had a chance in here," Brewster said. "How badly is Morse hurt?"

"He's dead. But the man who killed him won't live another day. That's a promise."

"Then why are you standing around here?"

Colin stepped out on the porch, slamming the door as he left.

"What do you want?" Brewster said to Oldring.

"Not a thing," Oldring said. And he, too, stepped outside.

Myra Chenoweth crossed the room to the chair in which she had been sitting when Gil Daly appeared. She leaned against the back of it and watched Brewster as he paced the floor. He had hardly glanced at her since she had come in. He seemed uninterested in her presence now.

"What about me?" Myra asked.

Brewster stopped his pacing. He glowered at her. He said, "You're our guest, Myra. You'll stay here for a while."

Myra tensed. "What makes you think so?"

"You'll stay," said Brewster.

He ran his hand over his head, still staring at her and seemingly puzzled about what to do. Then he nodded and left the room, but returned almost immediately with several blankets over his arm.

"I'm going to lock you in the root cellar," he said gruffly. "It's not too bad a place to stay. These blankets will keep you warm."

Myra bit her lips. She knew what a root cellar was like, how damp it was, how impossible it would be to get out. A feeling of hopelessness overwhelmed her. Gil Daly had managed to get away and was now riding south toward Logan's. He was counting on her to reach Antioch and tell the sheriff of Brewster's plan. He was counting on what help the sheriff could bring. But that help would never arrive. She had failed him.

"I'm sorry about this, Myra," Brewster was saying. "I'm sorry, but there's nothing else to do."

"You'll pay for it," Myra said, aware that such a hollow threat would gain her nothing, yet unable to hold the words back. "You'll pay for what you're doing."

"Men always pay for what they do," Brewster said, and there was a bleak note in his voice. "No one knows that better than I do. But sometimes, when you start something, you can't turn back, no matter what the cost. Would you rather stay here and give me your word not to try to escape?"

Myra shook her head.

"Come on, then," Brewster said.

He turned to the door, opened it, and stood waiting for her. And there was nothing for Myra to do but follow him.

116

CHAPTER
TEN

Before an hour had passed the moon came up into a cloudless sky, its pale radiance thinning the night shadows and widening Gil's range of vision. He had heard no sounds of pursuit and now looking back, he could see no one approaching. Near the Rhymer River he stopped to rest his horse and have a cigaret. Still looking back, he wondered what Dan Brewster would do. Myra could make it to town in another hour or so and wake the sheriff. By dawn, if they wasted no time, the sheriff and whatever men he aroused could be awfully close to Logan's. If Brewster was going to push his herd onto Logan's range and make his raid in the morning, he didn't have any time to waste.

And Gil had no time to waste. He rode on, fording the Rhymer River at a point below the crossing he had made as a member of the Swallowfork crew that headed this way to deal with a rustler named Farley. It was more hilly below the Rhymer River, and in every basin he passed he saw cattle. What the tally was on the Swallowfork, Gil didn't know. Frank Mills had once told him the Swallowfork ran close to ten thousand head. Certainly there was range and grass and water for

117

that many. This was as fine a cattle country as a man would ever see.

After another hour, Gil Daly angled to the west. When he came to Squaw Creek, he reined up. The southern boundary of Swallowfork was Dry Creek which, east of here and on across the basin, almost paralleled Squaw Creek. A strip of land, not much more than two miles wide, separated the two streams. This morning he had seen three men pushing a herd across Squaw Creek, not far east of here. It was this herd which Brewster had been planning to drive on south, across the border of his range, naming it a rustled herd the minute he did so, and following up with a raid on Logan's.

Gil turned east, following the course of Squaw Creek. He wanted to see that herd again. He wanted to see exactly where it was. He found it, all right, but not near Squaw Creek. The herd had been pushed on south through a fold in the hills. It had been pushed on across Dry Creek. It was already on Logan's range, and the three men driving it were driving it deeper. The excuse for a raid on Logan's already was an accomplished fact. Brewster could back down. He could change his mind in view of what Myra Chenoweth might be able to say. But he didn't have to, and Gil didn't think he would. He made a wide circle around the herd and rode on.

It was still shadowy dark when he pulled up in the yard at Logan's. There were no lights in the ranch house or in the bunk cabin beyond it. The horses in the corral had trotted up to the fence when he appeared, and seemed to be staring at him curiously, as though wondering why he had come. To the right of the corral was the low outline of the barn and a shed which almost adjoined it.

Gil sat crookedly in the saddle, resting for a moment, and trying to look ahead. He figured it was still two hours until sun-up, but if Brewster was coming, he wouldn't wait that long. He would strike in the first light of the dawn, maybe only a hour from now.

Still trying to look ahead, Gil rolled a cigaret. He was lifting it to his lips when he heard the rifle shot and felt his horse rear into the air. He sawed his horse down, swinging half out of the saddle, away from the house from where the shot seemed to have come.

"I can shoot straighter than that," call the high, sharp voice of Howard Logan. "Drop off your horse, mister, with your hands up. Or high-tail it for the hills."

Gil slid to the ground, lifting his arms above his head. "It's Gil Daly," he shouted. "I was here several nights ago with Max Sidwell."

The door to the house had opened just a crack. Moonlight glistened on the barrel of the rifle covering him. Gil stepped forward. The door opened wider and in its dark frame he could see the vague figure of a man.

"Are you the fellow who was looking for Pete Enders?" Logan asked.

"That's right."

The rifle barrel lowered. "Tie your horse to the corral fence and come on in," Logan said.

Gil caught his horse, tied him to the corral fence, and walked to the house. Lamp light now showed through the open door and as he stepped inside he heard Logan in the kitchen.

"I stirred up the fire," Logan said as he returned to the front room. "I put some water on for coffee. This is a hell of a time to call on a man."

"You seem to be up," Gil said dryly.

"I wasn't up," Logan retorted. "But these days, I sleep with one eye open. Coming back from the hills, you didn't happen to swing through the Swallowfork basin, did you?"

"I came here almost straight from Swallowfork."

Logan's eyes narrowed. His hand moved closer to his holstered gun. "Maybe you're still working for Swallowfork, huh?"

Gil chuckled. "Brewster would shoot you for saying that."

"Maybe. Or maybe not," Logan said, still suspicious.

"Then let me put it this way," Gil said. "I came here after a talk with Brewster. When I left him he was tied up and his men were taking shots at me. He had pushed up a herd north of here."

"I know about that herd," Logan said.

"Do you know where it is now?"

"On Squaw Creek."

"Wrong. It's only a few miles north of here. It's been rustled, Logan. By you."

Howard Logan sucked in a deep breath. "So that's his game, huh. And you're in on it with him."

The rancher's gun flashed out. He leveled it straight at Gil.

120

"Take it easy," Gil told him easily. "I'm not Swallowfork."

"How do I know you're not?" Logan countered. "I never saw you before the other night. You came here with Max Sidwell. You wanted to know where you could find Pete Enders but you didn't give any sound reason for wanting to find him. You were Swallowfork a week ago. Maybe you still are."

Gil Daly didn't know what kind of answer to make. He told himself he should have expected to run into something like this, for it was true that Howard Logan knew nothing about him. Added to that was the man's uneasiness and his deep distrust for Dan Brewster.

"Speak up, Daly," Logan was saying.

Gil nodded. He said, "All right, Logan. I'll speak up. You listen. Listen through to the end. Hold your gun on me if you want to, but pretty soon you'll need it for someone else."

Then, in brief, terse sentences, he told of his trip up Squaw Creek and what he had found and what he guessed. And of his visit to the Swallowfork and what he had learned there from Myra Chenoweth and Brewster. Toward the end of his story, Logan holstered his gun. When he had finished the rancher nodded grimly.

"So Brewster's got to prove he was right," he muttered.

"Right about what?"

"Brewster claims he caught a rustler who was working for me. He claims that two others who got away were driving his cattle. The sheriff tried to follow a trail Brewster's men pointed out. It didn't lead anywhere. But Brewster's got to be right. He's got to brand me as a rustler even if he has to do the job for me himself. You say Myra rode to Antioch to get the sheriff?"

"That was the plan."

Logan fingered his mustache. "The sheriff can't make it here before eight or nine. If Brewster's going to try anything, he'll try it before then. Maybe with his whole crew."

"How many men have you got?" Gil asked.

"Two. They rode in to town last night. Probably got drunk. They're not back yet. My wife is at her sister's."

"You mean you're here, alone?"

"That's the size of it, Daly. The door's over there. Your horse is outside."

Gil Daly thought it over. "Maybe we'd both better ride," he said finally.

"Not me," Logan said. "I built this house, Daly. Built it with my own hands, cut the timbers for it and put them up. I built the barn and the cabin my men use. I've got thirty years of my life in this place and in the cattle I own and in my land. Does a man turn his back on the work of thirty years?"

There was a stirring pride in the rancher's voice. The look in his eyes had sharpened and his stooped shoulders had straightened a little. He was growing old. He showed it in the lines in his face and in his graying hair. But the weight of years hadn't touched his spirit.

"How about that coffee," Gil suggested.

122

"If what you've told me is true, you'd better get out of here while you can," Logan said.

Gil stretched and appeared to relax. "I don't like to be hurried, Howard. Besides, your coffee smells good."

Howard Logan's shoulders seemed to shrug off a burden. He turned toward the kitchen, stepping briskly.

The first gray light of morning lifted slowly into the eastern sky. It had turned chilly. There was an icy touch in the wind which swept down from the Tetons. Gil finished caring for his horse, loosed him in the corral, then trudged on to the house. Inside, Logan sat in a chair near the window which looked out to the north. Leaning against the wall near him were two rifles. A second sixgun lay handy on the table.

"No sight of 'em yet," he said to Gil.

"Maybe Brewster will change his mind," Gil said.

But he didn't think so. Brewster's cattle were deep on Logan's range. His case was ready to be set. Whatever Myra might say he could discount as the emotional imaginings of a woman. Gil's support of her statements wouldn't stand up. Gil was a man who had been fired from the Swallowfork and who could be accused of trying to get even.

Out in the kitchen Gil poured another cup of coffee. He stood in the doorway between the kitchen and the front room, drinking it and studying Logan. Logan hadn't said much during the past hour. He had written something on a piece of paper which he folded and placed in his hip pocket. Possibly a note to his wife. After this, he had checked the loading of his two rifles and his two sixguns. Since then, he had been sitting at the window, staring out to the north, watching the dawn come up. And waiting for Brewster. Six or seven men might be riding with Brewster, but Gil had a notion that Logan would stay here if Brewster's crew numbered fifty. There was a rock-hard stubborness in the old rancher which he was only beginning to sense.

"Don't you think the sheriff could make it here by dawn, if he hurried?" Gil suggested.

"From the Swallowfork to Antioch and then over here is almost twice as far as you had to travel," Logan replied. "Nope, I don't think we can count on any help from the sheriff. In fact, I'm pretty sure we can't. Come here a minute."

Gil set his coffee cup aside. He moved up to the window.

"Look over that way," said Logan. "A bit to the left."

Gil peered through the window in the direction Logan was pointing. At first he saw nothing but the rolling hills, dotted here and there with cattle and spotted with occasional clumps of shrubbery and trees. Then, topping one of the hills and quickly dropping from sight, there was a group of riders. How many riders, he couldn't be sure.

"Five men," Logan said. "Only five. We're lucky."

Gil was aware of a sudden, sharp excitement. He loosened the gun in his shoulder, then glanced to where he had set the rifle.

"We'll let 'em ride up," Logan said. "Maybe Brewster will want to talk some. He usually does. He's a man who loves the sound of his own voice."

124

It occurred to Gil, belatedly, that he had no business here. He had quit his job at Swallowfork. On a hunch, he had turned back to find Pete Enders, figuring that if Enders had made a strike, he might be able to stake a claim for himself, a claim which would pay off faster than a cowhand's wages. That notion had still been in his mind when he found Enders' body and when he went to see Dan Brewster. It had been in his mind, all right, but he had gotten sidetracked. Sidetracked into a fight which was no concern of his at all. A scowl built up in his face.

"Here they come, Daly," Logan called. "Yep, five of them."

The old rancher was leaning forward in his chair, his face close to the window. His pipe was in his mouth but he hadn't lit it. His drooping mustache seemed to curl around the stem. Through the window Gil could now see the five riders quite distinctly. He marked the chunky figure of the Swallowfork foreman, Frank Mills. He thought one of the other men was Colin. And next to Colin rode the gaunt and stooped Lou Crowell.

"Brewster ain't with 'em," Logan said, and he sounded disappointed. "Now, I wonder why Brewster didn't come along?"

The five men drew steadily closer. They were walking their horses, now, about fifty yards away. They pulled into a brief huddle, then came on.

Logan got to his feet. He reached for one of his rifles and stepped to the door. He opened it just a crack. "Keep back from the window, Daly," he whispered. "Windows cost money. I want to save that one if I can."

Out in the yard in front of the house, the five men pulled up. Two moved quickly toward the corners of the house, passing out of the range of Gil's vision. The other three, Mills, Colin and Hondo, moved in closer. Colin and Hondo held rifles across their saddles. Mills leaned forward, his hat pulled low over his face.

"Hey, Logan!" he shouted. "Logan! Come out here a minute!"

Hondo had swung his horse toward the bunk cabin and was staring that way. Perhaps one of the men who had disappeared was also covering the bunk cabin. The other, at the corner of the house, might be covering the door. He would have a side shot at Logan, if Logan was foolish enough to step out.

But Logan didn't move out on the porch. "What is it, Mills?" he called through the crack of the door. "What do you want?"

"We want to see you a minute," Mills said. "We want to ask you a few questions."

"Ask your questions," Logan said. "Ask 'em now."

He poked his rifle through the open crack of the door. He lifted it, sighting along the barrel, and the men outside couldn't have failed to see it. Colin wheeled his horse away, shouting a warning at Mills and Hondo. Hondo streaked off in the other direction, but Mills hesitated. He hesitated, and then his arm snapped up, lifting the gun from his holster. He fired twice, and Logan, still at the crack in the door, seemed to shudder. He lowered his rifle, dropped it, and half turned toward Gil. There was a shocked and bewildered look on his face, and high in his shirt, at the shoulder, there grew a dark red stain. His lips stirred, but if he spoke Gil didn't hear his words. Then suddenly Logan's body folded. He sprawled to the floor and lay there, face down, motionless.

Through the window, Gil could see Mills hunched over the saddle and driving toward the corner of the barn. He whipped his gun up, smashing the old rancher's precious glass pane. He fired at Mills. He fired again. An answering rifle shot from the opposite corner of the barn drilled through the already shattered window pane. Gil dropped to the floor. He crawled to where he could reach out and touch Logan.

"Hey, old-timer," he said. "We're still in the fight."

But there was no response from Logan, no sign that he had heard. Gil inched closer. He rolled Logan over on his back. There was a glassy, uncomprehending emptiness in the rancher's eyes. The red spot on his shirt had widened to cover most of his shoulder. Gil crawled to the bedroom, and then back again. He spent the next few minutes fixing a tight bandage around Logan's shoulder, hoping to stop the flow of blood. How much good that would do, he didn't know. Logan seemed to be pretty badly hurt.

A score of shots had been pumped into the house from the men outside, but before Gil finished working on Logan's bandage, the shooting stopped. Now he edged closer to the door which was still open a crack. Through it, the yard seemed empty, but he could hear voices off to the left.

"No one in the cabin," Jim Oldring shouted. "If Logan's men are here, they're with him in the house."

"Then set the cabin on fire," Mills yelled back. "Hondo's taking care of the barn."

His voice seemed to come from the far corner of the barn. Gil reached for Logan's rifle. He lay where he was on the floor, waiting. A thin trail of smoke lifted from the corner of the barn. It grew heavier. It spread, pushing out through the chinks in the boarded wall. Hondo, mounted on his horse, made a dash from the corner of the barn toward the bunk cabin. Gil's rifle lifted, then lowered. He might miss a quick shot. He couldn't afford to miss. He heard a sound at the kitchen door. He turned and crawled that way. The kitchen door opened and he saw Lou Crowell in the entrance.

Almost at the same instant, Crowell saw him. The gun in the man's had swung toward him. Gil's rifle tilted up. He fired. Crowell gave one thin scream, and then Gil watched the man jerk backwards and stagger out of sight. He thought he heard him fall.

"They've got Crowell!" a voice screamed outside. Colin's voice. "The dirty bastards got Crowell!"

Bullets smashed through the kitchen door, raking above Gil's head. He levered another shell into the rifle. He turned back, and on his knees, took a quick look through the shattered window. Thick, dark smoke was now puffing up from the corner of the barn. Flames licked through it. He saw Mills racing his horse around the corral, probably to come up on the other side of the house. He crawled to the bedroom. Through the bedroom window he could see the bunk cabin on fire and beyond it he spotted Hondo and Jim Oldring, waiting there for Mills. He cut loose on them with the

128

rifle and saw Hondo throw up his arms and pitch from the saddle. Jim Oldring wheeled out of sight. A moment later he caught a glimpse of Mills. He fired, but Mills' rearing horse took the bullet, spilling the chunky foreman to the ground. He scrambled out of sight behind the burning bunk cabin.

It was two down now, and three to go. Hondo and Crowell were out of it. Mills, Colin and Jim Oldring still had to be dealt with. Gil mopped a hand across his face, and was surprised to discover perspiration. He stared through the bedroom window but could see nothing of Mills or Oldring. A few moments ago, Colin had been outside the kitchen. He might still be there — or had he gone somewhere else? He might even have entered the kitchen. There was a reckless streak in Colin Brewster, growing out of his determination to measure up to his father. It gave him no peace. He might try anything.

Gil scrambled back to the front room. From there he moved to the kitchen. Colin wasn't there. He returned to the front room and peered into the yard. The barn was fully ablaze. Neither the barn nor the bunk cabin would offer the three remaining Swallowfork riders any protection for very long. The crackling flames would excite their horses. The heat would be intense.

He glanced at Logan. The old rancher didn't seem to have stirred. He might even be dead. Gil remembered how Logan had talked about his ranch. He remembered the note of pride which had been in the old man's voice, the stubbornness he had sensed, the

129

quiet courage. His lips tightened. He watched sharply through the window.

"Hey, you fellows in the house," a voice shouted. Mills' voice. "This is only a taste of what anyone can expect who takes Swallowfork cattle. When you tell folks what happened this morning, tell them that."

Gil made no answer. There was no point in answering Mills' empty words. He hurried to the bedroom, for Mills' voice had seemed to come from that side of the house. He could see no one, however, from the bedroom window. Back in the front room a moment later, he caught a glimpse of the three remaining Swallowfork riders. They had turned away and were far beyond the blazing barn, swinging to the north. As he watched, they dipped from sight below a hill.

He stood up, again mopping his hands over his face. He checked the loading of the rifle in his hands, then set it aside. For another minute he stayed on guard, only vaguely conscious of the crackling sound of the fire which was consuming the barn. He couldn't see anyone now. The raid was over. But what Brewster had started wasn't over. It had only begun.

CHAPTER
ELEVEN

The sun was up and was an hour in the sky when Max Sidwell and the three men who worked for him came racing to the Logan ranch house. By that time, the barn and the bunk cabin were smoking ruins.

Gil Daly heard them coming and was out on the porch to greet them. He had shaved and eaten breakfast. He had done what he could for Howard Logan, it being impossible to ride for a doctor. Before leaving, one of the raiders had pulled down a back section of the corral, and the horses in it had fled from the flames.

"My God, man! What happened?" Sidwell shouted.

"You might look over there," Gil said bleakly. He pointed to the two blanket-covered figures on the ground near the porch.

Sidwell swung to the ground. He took a look under the blankets, then straightened, a tight, sober expression on his face. "Crowell and Hondo," he said slowly. "There were others, Gil?"

"Three others. Mills, Colin and Oldring."

"Brewster wasn't with them?"

Gil said, "No," but could add nothing to that. Brewster's absence puzzled him. Brewster had planned the raid. It wasn't like him to miss it.

"Where's Logan?" Sidwell asked.

"Inside. He's pretty badly hurt."

Sidwell entered the house. When he came back outside a few minutes later he was shaking his head. "It would be late afternoon before we could get a doctor here," he said. "I doubt if Logan lasts another hour. He says it was Mills who shot him."

Gil nodded.

"We saw smoke in the sky," Sidwell continued. "We got here as soon as we could." He ran his hands through his hair. "Tell me about it, Gil. How did you happen to be here? Where are the two men who worked for Logan?"

"The men who work here didn't get back from town last night."

"And you?"

Gil explained how he happened to be here. He told of his trip to Swallowfork last night and what he had learned from Myra. He mentioned the cattle which had been driven across Dry Creek as an excuse for the raid.

"So that was it," Sidwell said. Then he brightened. "Brewster will never in the world make a charge of rustling stand up. Myra Chenoweth can blast his story. So can you. He's gone too far this time, Gil. He's finished.

"Where does your sheriff stand?" Gil asked.

"Carl Huggins plays fair. If he was in Antioch when Myra got there, he ought to be here pretty soon. You'll see what I mean when he turns up. We'll be riding to the Swallowfork, all of us."

132

"We could ride now," said one of the men who had come with Sidwell.

The other two nodded, but Max Sidwell shook his head. "We'll wait for Carl Huggins," he said.

He and Gil went back into the house and stood at the door to the bedroom. Logan lay motionless on the bed, where Gil had carried him. His mouth had sagged open. He seemed to be staring at the ceiling. Sidwell crossed to the bed. He whispered the old rancher's name, but Logan didn't hear him. For Howard Logan, the fight was over.

Dan Brewster got up that morning while it was still dark. He prepared his own breakfast and ate it without pleasure. He hadn't slept well. In fact, he had slept hardly at all. Colin hadn't come in during the night, and this worried him. Myrna Chenoweth also worried him. He hadn't liked the necessity of holding her here. In addition to all this, he was bothered by what Gil Daly had said to him just before the fight started the night before. He couldn't make any sense out of it, yet it wasn't something he could put out of his mind and forget. If there was any truth in what the saddle bum had hinted at, old Pete Enders was dead, and his death was tied up in some way with the death of Bill Kemp and an assay report on the ore samples he had taken to Kemp. He hadn't known there had been any assay report.

It was just turning light in the east when Brewster left the house and crossed to Frank Mills' cabin. He knocked on the door and was answered almost immediately by Mills' wife. When she came to the door he handed her the key to the root cellar and gave her instructions about Myra's meals. She would follow them to the letter, he knew. Beth Mills was one person who never questioned what he did.

Fifteen minutes later he was on his way to Antioch and at mid-morning he pulled up in the yard in front of the corral. He left his horse there and started up the street, scowling, aware of a deep unrest. He could remember when he had enjoyed a trip to town. He had been able to look forward to it with pleasure. Any man he saw, he was glad to see, and most were glad to see him. But those days were long gone, now. He didn't like to come to Antioch any more. The town wasn't the same. Or he wasn't the same. Probably a little of both.

Moving on up the street, Brewster passed Charlie Weseloh, who nodded to him curtly. He passed two other men from the east fringe of the valley, but they were talking and didn't notice him. He came to Bill Kemp's office, pushed open the door, and stepped inside. Wes Olmstead, the young man who had worked for Bill Kemp, was seated at Kemp's desk. It was piled high with papers.

"Hello, Wes," said Dan Brewster.

Wes Olmstead scrambled to his feet. He was tall, thin, freckled, and had a shock of sandy hair and wide blue eyes. He said, "Hello, Mr. Brewster. I'm afraid you've come at a bad time. I'm trying to get things in order so Mrs. Kemp will know where she stands."

"Who's going to run the business for her?" Brewster asked.

134

"We have no idea," Olmstead replied. "I'd like to, if we can get things straightened around and there seems to be any chance to go ahead. But Bill kept so many details in his head, we hardly know where we stand."

"The day he was killed," Brewster said, "I left some ore samples here for him to look at. Any idea where they are?"

"Ore samples?" Olmstead repeated. He shook his head. "Haven't seen any ore samples in here since the last time Pete Enders came to town, months ago."

"You're sure of that?"

"Positive. I know ore samples when I see them. You're sure you left them with Bill?"

"Of course I did," Brewster snapped.

Wes Olmstead grinned. "I didn't know you were a prospector, Mr. Brewster."

"I'm not," Brewster growled. "But I left some ore samples here the afternoon Bill Kemp was killed. You weren't in that afternoon."

"I was looking at some cattle east of here."

"Did you find an assay report among Bill's papers?"

"A good many reports, but all of them old. Maybe Bill didn't get around to looking at the ore you brought in."

"He said he'd assay the stuff right away."

"Then he did. But — you know I wonder —"

"You wonder what?"

"The morning after Bill was killed I found the back door broken open. So far as I've been able to discover, nothing was taken, but if those ore samples you mentioned had any value —"

"They probably didn't,". Brewster cut in. "Forget it, Olmstead. It's not at all important."

He stepped outside, walked up the street, and in front of the feed store, stopped to take a cigar from his pocket. He bit off the end and clamped it tightly between his teeth, still scowling. He didn't like what Olmstead had told him. He didn't want to believe there was any value in the ore samples he had taken from Ed Farley.

But he had to be sure. He couldn't drop things here. In his own mind, Farley had been a rustler and his story of working with Pete Enders was a lie — a lie Farley had admitted before he did. That being the case, the ore samples couldn't have had any value, and wouldn't have been stolen. They should be around somewhere. Or at least Bill Kemp's report on his assay should be among his papers.

Gil Daly was just building up a story, Brewster told himself. The truth isn't in the man.

He crossed the street, walked around the bank, and five minutes later knocked on the door of Bill Kemp's home. Helen Kemp, who answered his knock, was a tall, fair-haired woman in the late thirties, and not unattractive. But she looked tired. Her eyes were red-webbed. She still didn't seem to have recovered from the shock of her husband's death.

"What is it, Mr. Brewster?" she asked, and there was no spirit in her voice.

"I hate to trouble you," Brewster said, "but on the day of Bill's death, I asked him to make an assay of some ore samples. I wonder if his report was in his pocket, or if he brought it home and it's somewhere around the house."

The woman shook her head. "There was no assay report in his pocket. I haven't found one around the house. Did you ask Wes Olmstead?"

"Wes Olmstead doesn't know anything about it."

"Then I wouldn't know what to suggest."

Brewster kneaded his bald pate with his hand. He didn't want to excite this woman. He didn't want to start any rumors, either. But he had to be sure of his ground.

"Could I ask you another question?" he said slowly. "Did Bill seem excited when he came home that night, the night he was killed? Did he say anything unusual?"

The woman frowned. "He told me someone was coming to see him later on. He didn't say who, or what it was about. Perhaps he did seem excited. I — I just don't remember."

"And you don't know who called him outside?"

"No. If I did —"

The woman's hands clenched. Tears glistened suddenly in her eyes. She retreated quickly into the house. And after a moment Brewster put on his hat and headed back toward town.

He had an early dinner at the Antioch House restaurant, sitting alone at one of the tables, struggling with the problem. After a too heavy meal he ordered a second cup of coffee. It was so hot it burned his lips. He set it down and as he looked around, he noticed Carl Huggins coming through the door and heading toward him. The scowl on his face deepened. Right now, he didn't want to have to talk to the sheriff, but he knew there was no escape from such a talk.

Huggins eased up to his table, pulled out a chair and sat down. He said, "Hello, Brewster. Mind if I join you for a minute?"

"Why not?" Brewster said. "You're already camped here."

Huggins placed his hat on the chair next to him. He dug his pipe from his pocket, filled it and lit it. He seemed tired. There were deep shadows under his eyes. His shirt showed sweat stains.

"I've just come back to town," he said. "I've been gone since yesterday. I'm going to tell you something, Brewster. Something I haven't told anyone else."

Brewster reached into his pocket for a cigar. He made no comment.

"I told you I was going to try to find out about Ed Farley," the sheriff continued. "I still can't prove he wasn't a rustler, but trying to find out about him, I ran into something else. From a couple men I learned where I might find old Pete Enders — at the headwaters of Squaw Creek. I took a ride up there. I found him, all right. He was dead. Murdered. His head had been crushed."

Brewster still didn't speak. He had a feeling that everything happening was closing in on him, hemming him into a tighter pocket.

"Funny thing," said the sheriff. "When I got to Enders' camp almost the first thing I saw was a rock cairn. There wasn't anyone around. I pulled the cairn down and under it I found the old prospector's body.

138

He looked like he'd been dead only a day or so. And then I noticed something queer. The rocks that had been piled over his body had been piled up real careful. They made a flat rock bridge over the old man's smashed head. It seemed like whoever covered his body wanted to protect the evidence of murder. Now what do you make of that?"

"What do you make of it?" Brewster countered.

"Several things," the sheriff said. "I looked around. I found the trails of three other men around the camp. One was old. I figured it might have been left by whoever had been working with Enders. Maybe Ed Farley. I'm not sure. The other two trails were more recent, so I figured this way. Two men rode up Squaw Creek, one behind the other, maybe one following the other. The first man killed Enders and left his body out in the open. Wild animals would soon have destroyed all evidence of the crime. But the other man, the one that followed, he built up the rock cairn. Built it up real careful so that when it was torn down anybody could see for sure that Enders died of a crushed skull."

Brewster lit his cigar. "What am I supposed to say now?"

"Well, I could figure this way," the sheriff said. "Someone from Swallowfork killed the old prospector to keep him from telling me that Ed Farley had been working with him."

"Then who built the rock cairn?"

Huggins tamped his pipe. "I don't know. There are lots of things I don't know."

"I don't know either," Brewster said. "And I don't know who killed Pete Enders. Do you want to take my word for it?"

"I'd like to, Brewster."

Dan Brewster jerked to his feet. He stared down at the lanky, stoop-shouldered Carl Huggins. He had seen the day when Huggins wouldn't have dared talk to him like this. What had got into the man? He didn't know. But like Charlie Weseloh, and Chenoweth, and Sidwell and Logan, the sheriff had turned against him.

Leaning forward, Brewster said, "Huggins, I didn't send anyone to kill an old man. I didn't do it myself. I don't work that way and you know it."

He turned abruptly toward the door. As he got there it came to him with a sudden force that Ed Farley, the man he had thought a rustler, the man he had ordered lynched, hadn't been a rustler. Farley hadn't been guilty of driving off Swallowfork cattle. His confession had been born of fear. In the matter of the death of Ed Farley, he was wide open to the charge of taking the law into his own hands. And Carl Huggins, when he could prove his case, would make the most of it.

It was well past noon. The thing to do now was to locate Gil Daly, if Daly still lived, and have another talk with him, find out just what he knew. And it might be a smart thing after that to take a ride up Squaw Creek himself and have a look at Pete Enders' camp. He might find something the sheriff had missed.

But Brewster didn't leave town immediately. Instead, he dragged up the street to the Teton Saloon, got his bottle and a glass from the bartender and moved to the

140

rear table. He poured and downed a short drink, then had another. He noticed the level of the whisky bottle: about half gone. He poured another drink and sat there, staring at it, trying to figure where things had gone wrong, where he had lost his grip. For that was what had happened.

He was still the boss of Swallowfork, but for a long time everything he had done had worked out wrong. Oh, he'd had his victories. After they made him blow up the dam he had built across the Rhymer River, he had still held up most of the water through the diversion of small streams to flood his meadows . . .

Yes, but to even the score, the men around Swallowfork had rustled his cattle and he'd never been able to prove this. The cattle he'd lost had been in handful lots, grabbed here and there. The sheriff had been no help to him in stopping it. In the best case he'd had to prove his point, two of his men captured Ed Farley, who wasn't a rustler at all but just a fellow who turned up in the wrong place at the wrong time. And now, on top of the lynching of Farley, he had the death of Tom Ash to worry about. And the kidnapping of Myra Chenoweth. And the murders of Bill Kemp and Pete Enders. And the return of Gil Daly.

Brewster finished the whisky he had poured. He looked around the room. There were several men in the Teton whom he knew, but no one had come back here to his table to join him. In the old days, he hadn't had to sit and drink alone. He lit another cigar, then stiffened.

Carl Huggins had come in and was striding toward him.

He eyed the sheriff warily. "Well, what is it?"

"Just one more thing," Huggins said. "After I rode down Squaw Creek canyon yesterday morning, I noticed where a good many cattle had been pushed south. I wondered if more rustlers were at work, so I took a look-see. The cattle were being pushed south toward Logan's by three of your men — Hondo, Crowell, and Frank Mills." Huggins sucked his teeth. "They were pretty close to Logan's range."

"But still on Swallowfork," Brewster snapped.

"Yeah, but it seemed a funny thing to me to push cattle so close to another man's range. What's the idea?"

"We graze our cattle where we want to."

It was a childish answer, and Dan Brewster knew it. It was a weak answer. He thought, There goes your beautiful plan, Mills. If Logan grabs the herd, Huggins will think we shoved them across the line ourselves.

He poured another drink. He heard the sheriff walk away. He heard laughter from the bar and the sound irritated him. He wouldn't accomplish anything by sitting here drinking. He knew that, but he was strangely reluctant to leave.

CHAPTER
TWELVE

At Logan's, Gil Daly chafed with growing impatience. The sun climbed ever higher into the sky, fast approaching mid-morning. An hour ago, Max Sidwell had ridden east to meet the sheriff, but by this time the sheriff should have arrived. If he had hurried, he was past due.

The three men who had come here with Sidwell still kept guard, just on the chance that the raiders might return. They loafed around, waiting, and pretty constantly watching the hills to the north, toward the Swallowfork. One, a man named Hugh Castlen, expressed the hope that they would come back, particularly Frank Mills.

"Why Mills?" Gil asked curiously.

"Mills is the man who killed Buddy Harper. That was about three years ago. The jury called it self-defense, and in a way I suppose it was. But in another way, it was murder. Buddy was just a kid. He couldn't begin to throw a gun with a man like Mills."

Castlen went on talking about the affair. He had been fond of Buddy Harper. He had tried to stop the fight, which had arisen over a bet made on a horse race, developed into angry accusations, and finally precipitated the tragic duel in which Buddy Harper had been killed.

Castlen's story ended with Buddy Harper's death, but it started Gil to thinking. In that single week spent on the Swallowfork, he hadn't learned to know Mills very well. His casual opinion of the man had been based only on what he had seen. It had been a rather negative opinion. He had seen Mills as a chubby, awkward man who loved his food, as a foreman without much authority, married to a colorless and unattractive woman; a man whose streak of meanness, shown sometimes in his attitude toward Colin, might be traceable to the frustrations in his life.

But to that bare picture, he could now add other details. It was Mills who had slapped Farley's horse from under him. It was Mills who took a hand in his own fight with Colin, smashing a gun down on his head. It was Mills who led the raid here at Logan's, and coolly shot Logan when the fight started. Yes, and before all that, Mills had killed another man here in the valley, a man named Buddy Harper. It was rather clear that his first opinion of Frank Mills could stand revision.

"I'm not the only one who would like to get Mills, either," Castlen was saying. "Talk to Joe Broomfield some day. Ask Broomfield why he don't like Mills. Broomfield has a ranch just north of Antioch."

Gil nodded absently and squinted to the east. There was no sign of the sheriff, or of Sidwell who had gone to meet him. Sidwell had suggested that perhaps the sheriff hadn't been in town when Myra arrived there, which might explain his delay. But Gil couldn't agree. He felt pretty sure that if the sheriff hadn't been in town, Myra would have stirred up a group of men on her own. She knew that Brewster might hurry his raid on Logan. She knew Logan would need help. If she had made it to town, she would have sent that help.

But she might not have made it to town. He hadn't seen her escape from the ranch. He had turned back inside the house, listened at the door, heard nothing, and assumed she had escaped. Or perhaps Brewster had ridden after her and caught her before she reached Antioch. That was a possibility, too.

"Castlen," he said abruptly. "Castlen, loan me you horse."

"Why, sure," Castlen said. "Sure. But what's bothering you?"

"I want to see what's holding up the sheriff."

The man nodded. "Go ahead, if you want to. It's my guess the sheriff's rounding up a posse. I'll have Mike or Scotty catch one of the horses that got out of the corral. There's an extra saddle on the back porch."

A few minutes later Gil Daly was riding east along the road which twisted through this hilly country below the Swallowfork basin. For several miles he stuck to the road, but finally, at a high point which gave a good view of the country beyond, he pulled up. Then for a time he waited, tracing the course of the road as far as he could see. Nowhere along it was there any lifting cloud of dust such as would have been raised by the posse. Max Sidwell having come this far, would continue riding until he got to Antioch. Sidwell would carry word of the raid to the sheriff. There was nothing to be gained by following Max.

But there was something else he could do. He had to face the fact that Myra hadn't reached Antioch. He could be sure of it. Why she hadn't made it to town, or what had happened to her, was a guess, but the answer probably could be found at Swallowfork. Carl Huggins, the sheriff, when he finally headed that way, would drive in boldly. He might be met with bullets or a cover-up argument. A man alone, slipping through the shadows as he had the last night, had a better chance than a sheriff's posse. A better chance, that is, if he wasn't discovered. A better chance if he played in luck.

Gil turned north, winding his way through the hills toward the Swallowfork. By noon he was out in the open country and by mid-afternoon he came to the Rhymer River. He stopped there, in the shelter of its bordering trees, sprawling on his back in the shade, and rested. He was beginning to feel the strain of the long hours he had spent in the saddle and of the hours he had gone without sleep. He was worried about Myra. A nagging guilt kept bothering him. He should have made sure she got away last night. He should have stayed with her during part of her ride to town. It hadn't been necessary to turn back and see Brewster. It had accomplished nothing.

The sun dropped down behind the Tetons. Gil stirred. He got up, flexing his muscles to drive the stiffness away. He untied the horse Castlen had loaned

146

him, swung into the saddle and rode on through the trees. Beyond them, he searched the rolling country intently. Cattle dotted the range everywhere but he could see no sign of horsemen. North and east, about two hours' ride from here, was the Swallowfork ranch house. It would be full dark long before he got there. It would be midnight before the moon came up. There might be someone on watch at the Swallowfork, all set to intercept the sheriff, but Gil doubted if anyone would be expecting a return visit from the man who had escaped the night before. They wouldn't think him that foolish. He checked his gun, rolled a cigaret, and rode north.

There were lights in the Swallowfork ranch house and lights in the bunkhouse. Gil paused at the edge of the grove, below and west of the barn. He stood there for fully five minutes, perhaps ten, his eyes probing the shadows, his ears straining for any unusual sounds. He saw nothing, heard nothing. He edged toward the barn. Before he was halfway there, the bunkhouse door opened. Framed against the lamp light inside, the chunky figure of Frank Mills was unmistakable.

Gil dropped to the ground. He lay there, watching. Mills said something to someone in the bunkhouse, then stepped outside and came straight toward the barn. He got his saddle and lugged it to the corral. He caught and saddled a horse. Then, after looping the reins over the corral fence, he turned toward the ranch house. He climbed to the porch, knocked on the door. A moment later, he stepped inside.

Gil hadn't been able to see who answered the door, but he thought it was probably Dan Brewster. He got to his knees, stood up and cut quickly toward the house. He stood there for a moment in its deep shadows, wondering how many men were in the bunkhouse. He had meant to find out before trying to see Brewster, but now there wasn't time. Not if he wanted to learn what Brewster and Mills were talking about.

Slipping around to the back porch, Gil climbed the steps down which he had fled the night before. He crossed the porch to the kitchen door, felt for the knob, turned it, and pushed. The door opened easily. Beyond it, the door to the front room was ajar. From the front room came the murmur of voices. Colin's voice, and Mills'. Gil stepped inside. He closed the porch door behind him. He drew his gun and stood listening. Mills was talking, right now, and there was an angry rumble in the man's voice.

"Who says I'm running out on you? I never ran out on anything in my life. It's a private matter that takes me to Antioch. What it's about is none of your damned business."

"A private matter," Colin said, and he laughed. "It's no private matter taking you to Antioch. You're not going to Antioch. You're clearing out before the sheriff gets here. You know as well as I do that he won't swallow the story that Logan rustled our cattle."

"And why won't he?" Mills demanded. "We drove that herd deep into his range. Who can prove he didn't do it?"

"Gil Daly can prove it. So can Myra Chenoweth."

"Gil Daly," Mills said, and he sounded disgusted. "You came riding south last night with some story of how Gil Daly had been here and escaped and how he went to warn Logan. If he did, what good did it do? If he talks himself blue in the face, who's going to listen to a saddle bum? As for Myra Chenoweth, she's still here, isn't she? Locked in the root cellar, how can Myra Chenoweth talk to anyone?"

Gil stiffened at the sound of Myra's name. He leaned forward, anxious not to miss a word.

"We can't keep her locked up forever," Colin was saying.

"Then marry the girl. You could do worse. Or turn her over to Jim Oldring. He's got ideas about her. He was asking me just now where he could get a key to the root cellar."

There was a moment of silence. Then Colin spoke again, his voice uncertain. "I wish the old man was here."

"The old man," Mills rumbled. "The old man. I thought you hated his guts. You were glad enough to help us rustle his cattle and pocket your share of the money. You thought you were big enough to stand alone. Why are you whining for him now?"

"So I'm whining for him, am I?" Colin's voice grew stronger. "I'm whining for him and you're running out. All right, Mills, run. But if you run, don't come back. We won't need you."

Gil heard the door open. He heard Mills' indistinct answer, and then heard the door close. A moment later, outside the house, a horse galloped away, its hoofbeats fading quickly into the distance. Frank Mills was gone. However many men were here, he had one less to worry about.

And he knew more than he had known a few moments ago. Swallowfork cattle had been rustled. Brewster was right in making such a charge. He had been wrong only in where he placed the blame. His foreman, his son, and probably some of his crew had been guilty of the rustling. It hadn't been the ranchers bordering on the Swallowfork.

From where he was standing, Gil could hear Colin pacing back and forth across the front room, muttering profanely under his breath. Colin was an unhappy man tonight. He wouldn't stay here very long. His nervousness, his indecision would drive him outside. But before that happened, Gil wanted something. He wanted the key to the root cellar. He took one careful step, another, a third. He reached the door to the front room. He pushed it wider, then all the way open. He lifted his gun in the same motion, covering the young man whose back was to him.

"Steady, Colin," he said. "Don't reach for your iron. It's all over if you do."

Colin spun around, his hand poised inches above his gun. But he didn't make a grab for it. He stared wide-eyed at Gil, his mouth sagging open. And then his lips formed the words, "You again." His voice mirrored the shock he was feeling.

"Yes, it's me again," Gil Daly said. "And you can hand over the key to the root cellar."

150

Colin straightened a little, his glance jerking from side to side, a scowl tightening on his face. Finally he said, "I don't have the key. I don't know where it is."

"Think fast," said Gil. "I want that key."

Colin shook his head. "I don't have it. But stick around, Daly. The old man will be back here after a while. He'll be glad to give you the key. He'll throw it right in your face."

Gil pulled in a long, slow breath. He knew the root cellar. The door was thick and heavy and fitted tightly into its frame. If locked, it couldn't easily be forced. He would have to have the key. He believed Colin knew where it was.

He walked toward the man. "One more chance, Colin," he said. "Give me the key."

Colin moistened his lips. "I don't have it."

Gil's arms whipped up and down, slamming the barrel of his gun at Colin's head. But Colin ducked, twisting away, clawing at his holster. He staggered under the blow on his head but his gun came out. Gil swung again. Colin's fingers tightened as his knees caved in, spilling him to the floor. The sound of the exploding bullet was loud.

Stooping over the man, Gil took his gun and dropped it into his pocket. Colin stirred, tried to get up. Gil tapped him again on the head.

Outside, someone was calling, "Hey, Colin. Colin, what's wrong?"

Gil straightened, his gaze circling the room. He stepped back to the kitchen and stood there waiting. Waiting for the man outside to come bursting in.

But the man stayed outside. He called Colin's name once more, then was silent.

Gil mopped a hand over his face, aware of the sharp tension in his body and of the quickness of his breathing. He had heard one man outside, but there might be more. If he ran, this could end in a repetition of what had happened last night. But he wasn't running. Not yet. He stood motionless a moment longer, a slender, tense figure, every muscle stiff, the gun in his hand ready. Then he darted across the kitchen, bolted outside and cut toward the east corner of the house.

A bullet ripped into the wall of the house just behind him, a bullet fired from the darkness beyond the house. Gil dropped to the ground. Another bullet sang past, high overhead. He saw the flash of the gun. He heard a voice screaming at him. Jim Oldring's voice. "You'll not get away this time, Daly. Throw down your gun and get your hands in the air."

The corner of the house was just ahead of him. Gil crawled that way, snaked around it, and then lay silent, waiting, looking back. He had heard a man out front just after Colin's gun exploded. He had been shot at by Jim Oldring from behind the house. There might be two men here; or maybe Oldring had been the man out front. Oldring might have hurried to the back of the house, guessing Gil would try to escape that way.

"Hey, Daly," Oldring was calling. "Daly, you're covered. Gorman's flanking me on one side, Mills on the other. You haven't a chance."

Gil strained his eyes against the darkness. He thought he could make out the crouching figure of Jim Oldring, but he wasn't sure. He edged away from the house, still watching. He saw the shadowy figure move. His eyes caught the dull glint of starlight on a gun barrel. He shoved his arm forward, steadied it . . .

Oldring must have spotted him at just that moment. Two shots blasted at Gil. Then a third.

Between Oldring's shots, Gil fired twice.

He heard Oldring's high, startled cry. The man's shadow reared up and came plunging toward him. Gil fired again. He saw Oldring stumble, saw him fall.

After a moment of anxious waiting, Gil moved cautiously to where the man lay. He stooped over him for a moment, then straightened up and holstered his gun. He would never have to worry about Oldring again. Excepting at night. Excepting in his troubled dreams. For things like this were never over. Things like this came back to haunt a man.

Back inside the house, Gil took another look at Colin, but Colin hadn't moved. There was a sound at the kitchen door. Gil jerked that way, startled, grabbing at his holster. But it was only Beth Mills who stood in the door, looking in at him, her face as expressionless as ever.

"Is Colin dead?" the woman asked.

Gil shook his head.

"But the one outside is."

"Yes, the man outside is dead."

"Which one was it?"

"Jim Oldring."

"He was no good," the woman said.

She was wearing an old brown sweater over a shapeless dress. She lifted one hand to brush at her hair. It was gray hair, stringy hair that never looked combed. She seemed older than Frank Mills. Much older.

"Do you know where I can find a key to the root cellar?" Gil asked abruptly.

"Why do you want it?" the woman asked.

"I want to get Myra Chenoweth away from here before Brewster gets back."

Beth Mills turned and left the room. She came back with a key in her hand.

"Hurry," she said. "You don't have much time."

Brewster had been wrong about Beth Mills. Like everyone else, Beth Mills had her moments of rebellion. This was one. A chance to do something she could later be proud of. She hadn't let the opportunity slip away.

CHAPTER
THIRTEEN

Gil crossed the yard at a run. He unlocked the door to the root cellar, pushed it open, and called Myra's name, half afraid there would be no answer. But there was. A shaky, whispered answer. "Gil! Gil, is it really you?"

He couldn't see a thing in the cellar's inky darkness, but he found her outstretched hands and pulled her closer, his arm dropping around her shoulders protectively. A blanket was wrapped around her. He could understand why. It was cold in the cellar. Cold and damp.

"I heard the shooting," Myra said, her voice still low. "I didn't know what to expect."

Gil was suddenly conscious of the way his arm had tightened around Myra's shoulders, pulling her close up against him, so close he could feel the warmth of her breath on his cheek. She would be twisting away in another moment . . . But she didn't. Through the folds of the blanket, Gil could sense the trembling of her body. Anger gathered in him, mingled with tenderness. Right at that moment Gil would have liked to hear Brewster riding up. He wished he could face Brewster now, before reason made him question the satisfaction of vengeance.

"Hadn't we better get away from here?" Myra said. "Or is it all over? Is the sheriff —"

Gil sighed. "Yes, we'd better get away. I'm afraid it isn't over, Myra. Where the sheriff is, I don't know."

They climbed from the cellar, Gil's arm still around her shoulders. They walked to the corral.

"I'll borrow a saddle from the barn," Gil said. "We'll catch you a horse. Mine's tied in the grove, like it was last night."

"You made it to Logan's?" Myra asked.

Gil nodded.

"And there was trouble?"

"We'll talk about it later."

He hurried to the barn, returning with a saddle, blanket and bridle. He caught one of the horses in the corral, threw the blanket and saddle on its back and fastened the cinch strap while Myra slipped the bridle into place. A moment later, riding double, they headed toward the grove. Above them, stars were bright in the sky. Behind them, soft lamp light showed around the curtained windows of the ranch house and bunkhouse and all seemed quiet and peaceful. But it was a deceptive quiet, a deceptive peacefulness.

Gil got his horse and they turned south, dropping far below the road which ran toward Antioch, and then swinging east. They avoided the road because they might meet trouble there.

"Tell me what happened at Logan's," Myra insisted.

Gil told her, stripping the story to its bare essentials. "It wouldn't have made any difference if you had reached Antioch," he concluded. "The sheriff couldn't

156

have made it to Logan's by dawn. That's when they hit us."

But Myra shook her head. "I had a chance to get away. I could have grabbed one of the horses at the corral after Colin and Oldring stepped out of the bunkhouse. But I waited, thinking they might go back inside. They didn't. They saw me. By that time it was too late."

She didn't say much more than that. She didn't speak of her struggle with Jim Oldring, or mention that he had tried to break into the root cellar earlier tonight. When the door opened, later, she'd been afraid it was Oldring again. The sound of Gil's voice, calling her name, had been like the answer to a prayer. But she kept this to herself.

They ran their horses for a while, then slowed down. Gil told her why he hadn't left the Rhymer River valley, and what he had found at the headwaters of Squaw Creek. He sounded a little defensive, as though he was afraid she might question his motives. "I went back to see Brewster the other night, just to let him know that I was onto his secret," he said. "Just to show him he couldn't get away with murder."

"And why did you ride to help Logan?" Myra asked, amused. "Why did you come back to the Swallowfork tonight."

"It's all a part of the same picture," Gil said. "What are you laughing about?"

"I'm thinking of what Brewster called you. I'm thinking of what I called you. A saddle bum. I was wrong, wasn't I, Gil?"

"Forget it," Gil said gruffly. "Maybe we'll not find. Pete Enders' strike. Maybe the claim I hoped to stake out close to it will prove worthless and I'll still end up broke."

Myra rode her horse closer to his. She reached out, resting her hand on his arm. "If you do, Gil, would you come to work with us? With Dad and me?"

Gil looked straight ahead. Something Myra's mother had said came back to him. They had been discussing how long it took to save up money at cowhand's wages. Kathy Chenoweth had mentioned a short cut, suggesting that he might marry some nice girl whose father owned a ranch. She said it lightly, aware that he was going away. But he hadn't gone away. He was still here.

"Would you, Gil?" Myra was asking, her hand still on his arm.

Gil pulled himself together. He said, "No, I don't think I would."

The words came out more harshly than he had meant them. Myra drew away, obviously offended or hurt. He searched his mind for something to add, something to take the sting out of his abrupt refusal. He muttered vaguely about being sure he would be able to make a stake up above the headwaters of Squaw Creek, but Myra didn't seem to hear him.

"Hadn't we better ride on?" she suggested. "It's still quite far to town."

So they rode on. The evening was still warm, the stars still bright, but something had gone out of the night. The warm and pleasant sense of comradeship

158

between them had disappeared. They were riding together, yet weren't together. Between them was a chasm Gil didn't know how to bridge, and wouldn't try to bridge. I had a place of my own once before, he told himself, and I didn't have to marry a girl to get it . . .

He reined up suddenly. Myra pulled in beside him.

"Two men," he said. "They're too far south to have come from Antioch. You can see them against the skyline."

Myra offered no comment. The two men were about a mile ahead of them and slightly to the north. They seemed to be riding in a direct line to the Swallowfork.

"Brewster, maybe," said Gil. "And Frank Mills. Only Mills said he was going to town, and would probably have stuck to the road."

Myra still was silent. And angry with herself. Angry that she should have felt hurt at what Gil had said a little while before. She took a quiet look at him now, sensing the tension in his body, and understanding it, or at least approaching an understanding. He was almost unknown here in the Rhymer River valley. There was no one to whom he could turn for help or who would vouch for him. It wasn't surprising that he should feel tense, or that he might snap an answer at her.

"Gil," she said, and she tried to put all the warmth she could into her voice. "Gil, what are we going to do when we get to town?"

"What are we going to do? Why, find out what happened to the sheriff, I suppose. And look up your father. He'll be worried sick about you."

"Not Dad," Myra answered. "He would be worried if he knew what happened, but when I left home he was building a fence which would keep him busy several days. He expected me to spend a night with Jean Rogers, or even two nights. I'm afraid I wasn't missed."

"You'd have been missed if I'd been working on your place," Gil said.

Myra laughed, and the uneasiness which had come between them was gone.

Dan Brewster was tired, but it was more a weariness of spirit than anything physical. This had been a day to remember, or more properly, a day to forget. And it wasn't over. He still had to face Mills and Colin and Jim Oldring. He still had to do something about Myra Chenoweth. He must look forward to what would happen tomorrow, but he didn't want to think about that.

He had been silent since he parted company with the sheriff and Max Sidwell and several other men south of Antioch. Gorman, who rode with him, had respected his silence. He wondered if Gorman could have told him any more than he did when he came into the saloon in Antioch and reported on the raid at Logan's. But he didn't question the man. They were cutting straight toward the Swallowfork. He would get at the truth when he faced the others. Mills and Oldring might lie to him. Colin might lie. But if Colin lied, he would know it. He had always been able to see through Colin's lies.

160

Looking back now, he mulled over how the sheriff and Max Sidwell had confronted him in the saloon at Antioch, charging him with the responsibility of the raid on Logan's. Warned of it by Gorman, who had been sent here by Mills, he had denied any knowledge of the raid, but added that his men had instructions to follow anyone caught rustling Swallowfork cattle, and to shoot them down if they could.

"If my men raided Logan, it was because Logan made a grab at Swallowfork cattle," he had told the sheriff. "If my men raided Logan, the proof of his guilt is on his doorstep."

There had been a brief wrangle about the herd the sheriff had seen being pushed south. Max Sidwell insisted the herd had been pushed onto Logan's range by the Swallowfork riders. But all the proof he could offer was what he had heard from Gil Daly. And Brewster had exploded at the mention of Daly's name.

"Who's this man Daly?" he had roared. "A saddle bum we hired, and fired when he couldn't do his job. A man who's bitter and wants to get even. Would you take Daly's word before mine? I've lived in this valley half of my life. Daly's just a drifter."

There had been mention of Myra Chenoweth, too. Sidwell said she had been kidnapped and was being held a prisoner at Swallowfork. But again, Max Sidwell relayed the story from Gil Daly, and Brewster challenged it, calling it ridiculous. And it did seem ridiculous that anyone would dare to kidnap Myra.

Then, quickly, before anyone could suggest riding to the Swallowfork to see, Brewster had volunteered to

161

ride south with the sheriff and Sidwell and anyone who wanted to go along, to check the story of the raid and the truth of Daly's assertion that it was the Swallowfork who had driven cattle onto Logan's range.

The sheriff had agreed, apparently discounting in his own mind the story of Myra's kidnapping. "We'll ride south," he said flatly. "We'll get the facts. When we get them I'll know what to do. I told you once, Brewster, that no matter what the cause, you couldn't take the law into your own hands. I meant it."

Brewster had been stalling, in his insistence on the ride to Logan's. He had fully expected to find himself under arrest before the day was over. Only through the chance of the disappearance of Gil Daly, and by his promise to bring Mills and the rest of the crew into town the next day, did he escape it. Gil Daly's disappearance had been the determining factor. Brewster had made a lot of it, discrediting most of what Gil had said to Sidwell.

Brewster straightened in the saddle. He stared ahead toward the lights in the Swallowfork ranch house, aware suddenly that he was almost home. Twisting in the saddle he glanced at Gorman. "Where do you stand in all this?" he asked gruffly.

"Why, I ride for Swallowfork," Gorman said.

"And what does that mean? Suppose we don't ride in to town tomorrow. Suppose a posse heads this way."

"I wear a gun, don't I?"

The answer was one he might have expected, and Brewster tried to feel a satisfaction in it. He didn't know that sometime during the night, Slim Gorman

162

would pack his stuff and head out of the valley, never to be seen around here again.

Colin came out on the porch as they were tying their horses to the corral fence.

"Find Mills," Brewster said to Gorman. "Tell him I want to see him. Oldring, too."

Gorman nodded and drifted away. Brewster turned, toward the house, anger lifting in his body. According to plan he was to be notified the moment Logan grabbed any Swallowfork cattle. He hadn't been notified. And in the back of his mind lurked the suspicion that his own men had driven the cattle across the line. It was a suspicion that he didn't dare examine too closely.

"Where have you been?" Colin growled.

"Shut up," Brewster said, "and come on inside."

He climbed the porch step and moved through the door. Colin followed him, slamming the door shut.

"Who told you to stage a raid on Logan?" Brewster demanded.

"That's not the point right now," Colin said. "Gil Daly was here again."

"Tonight?"

"A couple hours ago. He killed Oldring. He got away, Myra with him. They're probably heading for Antioch."

Brewster sucked in a deep breath. He tried to smother the exploding rage which swept over him, but couldn't. "And what were you doing while Daly was here?" he bellowed. "What was Mills doing? What kind of men do I have working for me?"

"Mills wasn't here," Colin said, his voice as harsh as Brewster's. "He left before Daly showed up. I did what you did when Daly had a gun on you. I didn't see any signs that you fought back the other night."

Brewster mopped a hand over his face. All this shouting was accomplishing nothing. And in anger, he would accomplish nothing. It was time to do some clear and fast thinking. If Gil Daly and Myra Chenoweth were on their way to Antioch, he might not have until tomorrow to come up with some plan. The sheriff, and as many men as he could stir up, might head for the Swallowfork tonight.

"Are you sure Daly and the girl left together?" he asked more quietly.

Colin nodded. "They left here together, all right."

"Where is Frank Mills?"

"He said he had to go to town."

"Why?"

"He wouldn't tell me. He said he had some private business in town. He was damned mysterious about it."

Brewster's eyes narrowed. He had done a lot of thinking about who might have killed Bill Kemp, and who later might have made the trip up to the headwaters of Squaw Creek and killed Pete Enders. He spoke a name under his breath. The name was Frank Mills. He built up his case against Mills. Mills had known of the sack of ore he'd taken to Bill Kemp and might have discovered the results of the assay. Mills had been in town the night Kemp was called to his door and shot down. The night Pete Enders was killed, Mills had been south of here, presumably helping Hondo and

Lou Crowell push up the herd for Logan to rustle. But Mills might not have been with them. He could have taken a side trip up Squaw Creek canyon.

"Colin," Brewster said abruptly, "what do you know about Pete Enders?"

"Why, he's an old prospector. Farley, that rustler we lynched, said he had been working with him."

"Farley told the truth," Brewster said.

Colin looked frankly puzzled, and Dan Brewster, watching him closely, felt an immediate relief. For the first time since early morning the tension in his muscles relaxed. He could be sure of one thing, at least. Colin hadn't been mixed up with the death of Bill Kemp or Pete Enders. Colin was in the clear so far as those matters were concerned.

"I don't get it," Colin was saying. "What do you mean about Farley telling the truth?"

"Just that. He wasn't a rustler. He had been prospecting with Enders above the headwaters of Squaw Creek. The ore samples I took in to Bill Kemp showed a good color. Someone guessed that before I did. Someone shot Bill Kemp to death to keep him from spreading the news, and stole the assay report and the ore samples. The same man rode to Pete Enders' camp three nights ago and killed him."

"Mills?"

"Why do you say Mills?"

"It fits," Colin said. "That's all. It fits, damn him."

"You were ready enough to follow him this morning, Colin."

Sensing the critical note in his father's voice, Colin grew defensive. "I never liked the man and you know it. I've told you a hundred times we ought to get rid of him."

"He pushed our herd across Dry Creek, didn't he?"

"Sure, he pushed them across. That's the kind of man he is. I've warned you against him before."

Dan Brewster swallowed painfully. He could still feel grateful that Colin hadn't been involved in the deaths of Bill Kemp and Pete Enders, but that didn't change the picture a great deal. Myra Chenoweth had been held here a prisoner. A raid had been made on Logan's, a raid he couldn't justify. Logan was dead. Those things he would have to account for before another day passed. And he could see no way out.

Colin checked his gun, shoved it back into its holster and turned to the door.

"Where are you going?" Brewster asked.

"After Frank Mills."

"He can't get away," Brewster told him. "If he knows where Enders made his gold strike, he won't want to."

"I'm still riding after him," Colin said. "I've got a few private matters to settle with your foreman."

He slammed the door as he left the room.

Alone in the house where he had lived so long, Dan Brewster paced back and forth across the floor. He needn't worry about the death of Bill Kemp or the murder of the old prospector. Mills would have to answer for that. But in everything else, the responsibility was his. It was his men who had lynched Farley, his men who had pushed Swallowfork cattle across Dry

Creek and followed up with a raid on Howard Logan's. It was at his orders that Myra Chenoweth had been kept here against her will.

He was in a corner, hemmed in on every side. It didn't matter that he had been pushed here or that he had wanted things to work out differently. All that counted were the results men could see.

He crossed the room and slumped into his chair, his head sagging forward on his chest. A big man, thick-bodied, powerful. A man who ordinarily knew his own mind, but who tonight was tortured by indecision. He looked up when he heard Colin riding away. He got to his feet and started toward the door. By the time he reached the porch he was running, one thought driving through his head. Colin was no match for Frank Mills. Against a man like Mills, Colin wouldn't have a chance.

CHAPTER
FOURTEEN

It was after midnight when Gil Daly and Myra Chenoweth reached Antioch. They came in from the southeast, following the road which dropped down toward Max Sidwell's and Howard Logan's ranches.

"You'll want to talk to the sheriff as soon as you can find him, won't you?" Myra said.

"I think it's time I did," Gil said. "For all I know he may be hunting for me. What kind of person is he?"

"A good man. A little cautious, maybe. If Max rode in and told him what had happened at Logan's, he'd want to check the story and see for himself."

"And when he did, what then?"

"Why then he'd probably head for Swallowfork."

"So we might not find him here."

"We might not."

They rode down the main street. The night was still dark. There was no moon yet in the sky to add to the pale light of the stars, but ahead of them, lights showed through the windows of several saloons, and six or eight horses were clustered at the hotel tie-rail. At least part of Antioch was still awake.

Up near the bank corner, the door of a house opened and in the soft yellow glow of lamp light, Gil saw a man step out on the porch. He was short, chunky, almost fat. His hat was pulled low on his forehead. Gil had one clear glimpse of him before he stepped away from the door and into the shadows of the porch.

"That's Mills," he said. "Frank Mills."

Myra reined up. "Are you sure, Gil?"

"I'd know him any place. And that house —"

"It's where Carrie Hawes lives."

Gil nodded. He had stopped at that house to talk to Carrie Hawes, the daughter of Pete Enders. He'd had a good reason for wanting to talk to her, and perhaps Mills had the same reason. He recalled, now, that before leaving Swallowfork, Mills had told Colin of a private business matter he must attend to in town.

"Are you thinking what I'm thinking?" Myra asked.

"Probably."

"It could have been Mills who knew about the assay report. It could have been Mills you followed up Squaw Creek canyon."

Gil Daly was revising some of his opinions. He could have been wrong about Brewster. Mills might be the man who had killed Bill Kemp and crushed the head of old Pete Enders. And perhaps he didn't have the secret of the gold strike. What other explanation was there for this late night visit to Carrie Hawes?

"You wait here," he said to Myra.

"No, Gil. The sheriff —"

But Gil was already moving ahead, his gun clutched in his hand. He pulled up in front of the house where he had seen Frank Mills. The door was closed. There was no chunky figure lurking in the shadows of the

169

porch. Mills must have stepped to the far corner of the house and turned toward the back.

Gil couldn't see him, couldn't see anything in the dark area between the two houses, or beyond. He swung to the ground, trailing the reins of his horse. Myra had ridden after him and he heard her calling, "No, Gil. Let him go. Let the sheriff ride after him."

"I'm just going to take a look," Gil answered.

He hurried to the front corner of the house, stopping when he got there, and peering ahead. Mills, looking up the street, could have seen him and Myra, and might have guessed who they were. Such a possibility was something to think about. If there was any truth in it, the chunky man might not have hurried away. He could be hiding somewhere in the darkness, waiting, gun drawn and ready.

Gil stalked into the shadows, his ears straining to catch any unusual sound. He reached the rear corner of the house. From there he could see the shed in the yard, and against it a wood pile, and to one side a wagon. Some distance beyond the shed loomed the dark shadow of several houses. But in all this wider area he saw no sign of Frank Mills.

The shed was the nearest hiding place. Gil angled that way, running, hunched over. He heard the roar of a shot. He saw the muzzle flash from the corner of the shed, and it seemed to him that he could feel the breath of the bullet against his cheek. He dived to the ground, rolling away from the spot where he had fallen. He heard another shot, and another. Sand kicked into his face. He lifted his gun and fired, driving a shot straight

170

at the shed corner where he knew Mills was standing. He rolled away again, then lay motionless, hugging the ground, his gun slightly lifted.

The next minute was one of the longest he had ever known. He didn't dare risk another blind shot. Mills, crouched and waiting at the corner of the shed, would see the explosion of his gun and could fire at its flash before he could roll away. But there was something else to worry about, too. Although flat on the ground, he was out in the open. Mills, searching the ground for him, might be able to identify the dark shadow of his body. Given time enough, Mills might not need the flash of his gun to aim at.

A trickle of perspiration ran down the length of Gil's outstretched arm. His whole body felt clammy. His breath was coming faster. He felt the pressure to do something, to bait Mills into another shot, to drive him into the open before it was too late. But any movement of his own might be fatal. There was nothing to do but lie here. Lie here and wait.

Back of the shed there was a sudden creaking noise and then immediately the sound of hoofbeats. Gil jerked quickly to his feet, and started running, swinging in a circle toward the rear of the shed. He knew what those sounds meant. Mill's horse had been tied behind the shed. Mills had waited for a shot at him, but wasn't waiting any longer. He had drawn back, mounted his horse, and was wheeling away.

Gil got one more shot at a bobbing figure crouched so low over the saddle as to be almost part of the horse's bulk. He meant to fire again, but the thick night shadows closed in over Mills like a curtain. In another moment even the sound of the horse was swallowed up in the darkness.

Gil blew through the barrel of his gun, reloaded it, and slid it into its holster. After a moment he started retracing his steps to the house.

"Gil!" Myra called. "Gil, you're all right?"

She came hurrying toward him from the back corner of the house, and to Gil, it seemed like the most natural thing in the world to take her in his arms and hold her tight.

"Of course I'm all right," he said, keeping it matter-of-fact.

"You do the craziest things," Myra said.

Her arms were under his, her hands on his shoulders. She looked up at him and even in the darkness Gil could see the smile on her face.

"This is crazy, too," he muttered. And leaning down, he kissed her. It was a quick and blundering kiss, but there was something nice about it, a sweetness and tenderness Gil would remember.

Myra pushed him away. "There will be all sorts of people around here in a minute. The shooting will bring them."

She sounded breathless. She lifted her hands and started fussing with her hair, making sure the braids were in place.

Gil swore soundlessly, disgusted with himself. He hadn't meant to kiss Myra. It was just something which had happened. So far as Myra was concerned, it was all right, but that statement of her mother's still bothered him.

"We'd better walk around in front," Myra said.

She hurried toward the corner of the house. Gil caught up with her and together they walked back to the street.

Three men were standing in front of the Toltec Saloon. Two more were about to join them. The men were staring in the direction of the Hawes house, but the crowd which Myra had predicted didn't seem to have gathered.

"Where's that big audience you promised?" Gil asked, grinning.

Myra shook her head, puzzled.

Gil offered his own explanation. "Most folks don't go charging off into the darkness when they hear shooting. The sheriff probably would. Since he hasn't, its my guess he's not here. How well do you know Carrie Hawes?"

"Fairly well."

"Let's go in and talk to her."

They climbed the porch and knocked on the door. They had to knock several times before the woman's voice answered from beyond the door. A frightened voice, begging them to go away. But Myra gave her name and insisted that Carrie let her in, and after a moment Gil heard the clicking of a bolt and saw the door pull open.

"We want to talk to you just a minute, Carrie," said Myra. "A friend is with me. Gil Daly."

The woman wasn't holding a lamp this time. Gil couldn't see her in the darkness of the hall. "What do you want?" she asked hesitantly.

"Can't we come in?" said Myra. "You won't mind Gil. And we won't stay long, I promise."

"But it's almost morning."

"I know it is, Carrie, and I'm sorry. But you were up, anyhow. Someone was just here."

"That's not true," Carrie said.

"There wasn't anything wrong in it," Myra said soothingly. "The man was Frank Mills. He was questioning you about your father, wasn't he?"

Gil heard the sound of the woman's quick indrawn breath. "He told me he found my father after the accident, and before he died. He said he had a message for me, but it wasn't much of a message. Come on in and close the door. I'll light a lamp."

Her footsteps moved away. Gil leaned forward and touched Myra on the shoulder. "Nicely handled," he whispered.

A flicker of light streaked into the hall from the front room, then brightened as the lamp chimney was settled down over the wick. Myra and Gil stepped into the hall, Gil pulling the door shut behind him. He followed the girl into the front room.

Carrie Hawes stood near the table, a short woman, thick-bodied, middle-aged and haggard. Her dark dress was buttoned high at the throat, its skirts sweeping the floor, a costume in marked contrast to the jeans, shirt and coat worn by Myra Chenoweth.

"This is a fine time for anyone to be out," said Carrie Hawes, disapproval in every word.

"But we can't help it any more than you can," Myra said.

"And that shooting outside," Carries went on. "It sounded like it was right behind the house."

Myra took her by the elbow. She said, "Carrie, do you mind telling us what message it was Mr. Mills brought from your father?"

The woman freed her arm. "I said it wasn't much of a message. It wasn't. It was just that Dad hoped I'd get along all right and that he was sorry he hadn't been able to do more for me." She bit her lip and then added, "I reckon he meant it, at that. Dad was always talking of what he would do for me when he struck it rich. He was always dreaming crazy dreams of the things he'd buy me."

"Did Mills leave right after he gave you the message?" Gil asked.

"No. He wanted to know if I hadn't received a letter or a note of some sort from Dad. He kept insisting I had, though. I don't know how it would have been possible. There's no place Dad could have mailed a letter from the Tetons. And he was never a hand at writing except in his record books."

"His record books?" Gil said.

The woman nodded. "Dad kept a record of every prospecting trip he ever made. I have a dozen of his books, filled with drawings of the hills and cross marks showing where he took ore samples, and a word or two of comment about each sample, and the date."

"You mentioned those record books to Mills?"

"I did. And he asked a lot of questions about those books which were none of his business."

"Questions such as what?"

"Well, he wanted to know where Dad kept his book when he was out prospecting. He wanted to know if he wrote in it every day. He wanted to know how big the book was. If you ask me, your Mr. Mills was more interested in Dad's record book than he was in bringing me his message."

Gil agreed completely. He could have told this woman, in all honesty, that her father hadn't sent her any last message after an injury. He had seen Pete Enders' body and, from the way the old man's skull was crushed, knew he had died instantly. Mills had made up the message, using it as an opening wedge for his questions.

"Why do you think Mr. Mills was so interested in those little books Dad was always writing in?" Carrie asked.

"Because one — the last one — might have been of value."

"You mean —"

Gil shook his head. "Don't hope too much, Mrs. Hawes. But there's a chance, just a chance, that your father did make a strike up there in the Tetons."

"Then he —" The woman's voice broke off. Her eyes widened. She was staring past Gil toward the hall door.

Gil swung around. He had heard no warning sounds at all but two men stood in the doorway, guns covering him.

176

"I reckon your name's Daly," said one. "If it is, just stand there, peaceful like."

Gil raised his hands shoulder high. He didn't know these two men. He had never seen them before.

"Hello, Eddie," Myra said. "Hello, Mike."

She came over and stood at Gil's side, smiling at the men. She had been hidden from them by the door, and at the sight of her, both seem startled.

"Myra!" The shorter man gulped. "But we thought — that is, from what we heard when we rode in, just a little while ago, you're supposed to be at Swallowfork. At least, the sheriff figures things that way."

"He must be wrong," Myra said.

"And this fellow Daly —"

"What about Gil Daly?"

"Well, we don't know much about him. Again, from what we heard, maybe he stood up with Logan, this morning. Or maybe he rustled Swallowfork cattle and tried to pin the blame on Logan. The sheriff sure wants to see him."

"Where is the sheriff?" Gil asked.

"On the way to Swallowfork. He left maybe an hour and a half ago, soon as he heard Myra wasn't home. Quite a crowd was with him. Your father was one, Myra. We got here too late."

"If there's any trouble at Swallowfork, you can still get there in time for it. That is, if you don't fool around."

The two men glanced at each other. "You really think so?" asked the taller.

"Yes," Myra said. "And don't worry about Gil Daly. He got me away from Swallowfork."

There was more talk, but it didn't run on very long. Myra accompanied the two men to the door, complimented them on the courage they had shown in coming here to defend Carrie Hawes, and sent them running for their horses. They would try to catch up with the sheriff, but they wouldn't make it.

"You can do other things besides ride, can't you?" Gil said, joining Myra at the door.

"I can even cook," Myra announced.

They said their farewells to Carrie Hawes and walked out to their horses.

"Where will you go?" Gil asked. "Could you stay with Jean Rogers tonight?"

"I could, but I think I'll ride up to the ranch. Mother will be worried. After sun-up, I'll come back to town. Gil, would you ride there with me?"

"I've dodged the sheriff too long, Myra. I think I'd better wait in town."

"We could get back before the sheriff."

"Maybe. But I think I'll stay here. I don't want to seem to be ducking out again."

"I could stay too," Myra offered.

She put out her hand, rested it on his arm. She was gazing at him as though trying to read in his face what he wanted her to do.

"Up with you," Gil said. "We can't have Kathy worried. I can get a room at the hotel."

"Then ride with me that far."

Gil boosted the girl into the saddle, mounted his own horse and rode with her down the street. They pulled up in front of the hotel. Myra stretched out her hand. Gil took it.

"I haven't tried to thank you," she said. "I haven't, but I will."

"You don't have to thank me," said Gil. "Some things, people do because they want to. Anyhow, I'll be around."

"That's a promise?"

"Yep." He squeezed Myra's hand, let it go, and sat watching as she headed up the street.

But after the darkness had swallowed her, he didn't dismount and enter the hotel. Instead, he turned back in the direction from which they had come. South of town, he swung east. He had been doing some thinking. The sheriff and a posse were on the way to Swallowfork. They might find Brewster and Colin but certainly not Frank Mills. Mills, after what he had learned from Carrie Hawes, would head for Squaw Creek canyon and search for old Pete Enders' record book. It was Mills whom the sheriff wanted, but the sheriff didn't know it.

Well, Gil Daly knew about Mills. He nudged his horse into a mile-eating trot.

CHAPTER
FIFTEEN

Colin didn't slow down until his horse was winded. He didn't want to slow down then. A driving impatience was nagging him. Finally, and in no uncertain terms, he was going to come to an understanding with Frank Mills. He had been used by the man for the last time. He had played a waiting game too long. The time for waiting was over.

After too brief a rest, Colin rode on, still heading toward Antioch.

But an hour along the road he slowed down once more, a new thought troubling him. Right now, he wasn't going to be very welcome in Antioch. Or Mills either. Or anyone else from the Swallowfork. For a while, probably, people were going to be pretty much upset over what had happened at Logan's this morning. In fact, Mills might run into some of Logan's friends and end up sorry he had come to Antioch.

Colin grinned at that possibility, deciding it was just what Mills deserved. Mills always had been too sure of himself. Too clever. Too damned clever. He could he as casually as he could tell the truth, and he could make the lie stick, no matter how big or how little.

The grin which had come momentarily to Colin's face was gone. He was scowling, struggling with another troublesome idea. Before leaving Swallowfork, Mills had said he was going to Antioch on some private business. He had saddled his horse and left. On a dozen other occasions which Colin knew well, he had heard Mills say to his father that he was going to some specific part of the Swallowfork basin when he knew Mills planned to go somewhere else. And knew why. His father had accepted the blunt and easily told lie without question, just as he, right now, was assuming that Mills had gone to Antioch.

Here was something to think about. Colin pulled up. He rolled and lit a cigaret and stared through the darkness. Why would Mills go to Antioch? He could think of no good answer. What was the private business which called him there? He could think of none. But he could figure something else. From what his father had told him, Mills had killed Bill Kemp and stolen an assay report, then had killed old Pete Enders. Mills knew the secret of the old prospector's strike. He hadn't had time in the last few days to do much about it, but the days ahead were ideal to take off for such a purpose. Mills could step out of the way and let Dan Brewster face the trouble which would result from the raid on Logan's. Mills hadn't gone to Antioch. He had headed for Squaw Creek canyon.

The more he thought about it, the more Colin felt sure he was right. Or even if he was wrong, the one place Mills would soon show up was at the old prospector's camp. He could be certain of that. If he didn't find Mills there, he could wait and let Mills come to him.

Colin laughed, suddenly quite pleased with himself. He left the Antioch road and swung southwest toward Squaw Creek. A few minutes later, Dan Brewster, who had been following him, passed the place where he had turned off the road, and continued on to the east. But Colin didn't know his father had left the ranch.

It was dawn when Colin reached the Squaw Creek line shack. He stopped there for a time to make his breakfast from the cache of supplies in the shack, and to choose some food to take with him up the canyon.

Then he rode quickly on, and in the canyon, spent a little time searching for a recent trail. He couldn't find one and this annoyed him. It meant his analysis had been wrong and that Mills hadn't headed this way last night. But his other guess might still be good. Though Mills hadn't come here last night, he would show up here eventually.

Sure of this, Colin continued up the canyon trying to avoid the bare spots here and there where his horse's hoofprints might be noticed. He made good time and by mid-afternoon came out on the plateau, near the headwaters of the creek. He had never been here before but he soon located old Pete Enders' camp and saw the cairn of rock in front of it. The stench of decaying flesh told him what was under the cairn. He didn't disturb it. Near by, hidden from the camp by a screen of shrubbery, he settled down to wait, his horse tied deeper in the trees.

182

He didn't have long to wait. So soon that it startled him, he heard the sound of hoofbeats, and a moment later he saw Frank Mills ride into the camp's clearing. Mills, apparently, had no thought that anyone else might be near. He dismounted, tied his horse, and hurried to the crude shelter Pete Enders had built up against the wall of the cliff. He stepped inside, out of Colin's sight.

A minute passed. Another. Another. What Mills could be doing in the shelter, Colin couldn't guess. He had taken a look inside himself and had seen only a pile of blankets and a war-bag, probably stuffed full of dirty clothing.

At last Mills came outside and stood staring at the rock cairn. A short, stocky man. Brooding and muttering under his breath. He reached out suddenly, lifted one of the rocks from the cairn and tossed it aside. Then another, and another. Deliberately, angrily, he was tearing down the cairn.

Colin watched, fascinated, unable to guess what was in Mill's mind. When the old prospector's body was fully exposed he saw Mills reach into the trousers pockets and then the coat pockets. He didn't seem to find anything. Or at least, he didn't seem to find what he was searching for. Again, muttering something indistinguishable, Mills stood up. He reached out with his boot and poked the old prospector's body and started swearing.

Colin stood up. He loosened the gun in his holster and stepped around the shrubbery behind which he had crouched.

"What's the matter, Mills? Couldn't you find it?"

Mills whirled catlike to face him, his chunky body doubling over, his hand sweeping back to rest on his gun. But Colin's gun was covering him, and Colin's voice cracked at him with a grating harshness.

"Don't try it, Mills. Don't try it."

For an instant, Mills held his tense pose. His sharp, dark eyes burned at Colin. His lips were drawn back tightly against his teeth. Then, in a startling change, his body relaxed and he straightened up, laughing.

"You sure startled me that time, Colin," he said easily. "I didn't think there was anyone around here."

"I'm here," Colin said. "Count me in, Mills. Count me in all the way."

"All the way?" Mills said, and he sounded puzzled. "What do you mean by that?"

"Just what I said. Do you remember a talk we had about a year ago, up on Four Mile creek?"

"We've had lots of talks up there," Mills countered.

"But not like the one I'm referring to. I had the whip hand then. I knew you and some of the others were rustling the old man's cattle. I knew who was working with you on the outside. I could have had you booted off the place, and you know it. Instead, I was fool enough to throw in with you."

"It wasn't such a fool idea at that," Mills said. "You needed extra money, needed it bad. You couldn't go to your old man for it. The cattle we rustled didn't hurt him any but it gave you a nice side income."

Colin winced inwardly. That was true. He had needed money badly when he threw in with Mills. But he should have had Mills and Crowell and Hondo thrown off the Swallowfork. He should have made his father give him the foreman's job. When he needed extra money he could have arranged it through the same kind of deal. And it wouldn't have been stealing, since some day all of Swallowfork would be his. The mistake he had made a year ago, he wouldn't repeat now.

"I've got the whip hand again, Mills," he told the man.

"I still don't get it, Colin."

"Then let me put it this way," Colin said. "Farley wasn't a rustler. His ore samples assayed high. You got Kemp's report. You killed him. You killed the old man lying there after you found out where Farley's ore samples came from. Now do you get what I mean when I say I'm in this all the way?"

"That's a lot of brave talk, Colin. What can you prove?"

"All of it."

Mills eyed him carefully. "I don't believe you, but I reckon it's not important. We can work things out, Colin. Put up your gun. You don't want to kill me before I tell you where the gold strike is. And I don't want to kill you. I'm going to have to have someone to front for me. That raid we made on Logan's has got the whole valley stirred up, just as I was afraid of."

Colin stared at the gun in his hand. After a moment he slid it into his holster. "I can jerk this gun out again awfully quick," he said. "Don't try anything, Frank."

"I'm not going to try anything," Mills said. "Let's sit down and talk."

Colin trailed Mills to the far edge of the old prospector's camp. It was higher up here, and from where he was standing he could see above the trees and shrubbery and mark the point where the canyon walls came together and the trickle of the creek started its winding way to the lower Swallowfork basin.

"Old Pete picked a good place to hang out, anyhow," Mills commented. "The wall of the canyon gave him protection against the weather, and from here he had a view of the canyon opening in case he was worried about visitors."

"It doesn't seem to have done him much good," Colin said. "Where did he make the strike?"

"At a point about five miles from here. On up the canyon in a blind draw. We'll ride that way later on."

"And what were you hunting for when you came here?"

"A record his daughter said he kept. We don't have to have it, of course."

"We?"

"Of course, Colin. You and me. Why not? We need each other."

Colin Brewster said nothing, but he had his own ideas about that. He was fed up with Frank Mills. He needed the man, but only until Mills showed him where the gold had been found. Out of the corner of his eye he watched Mills get his rifle, set it against the cliff, then squat down near it.

* ★ *

Gil Daly was well across the basin by the time the sun came up. He hadn't traveled too fast. His horse was pretty well worn down, and to be honest, he was too. It seemed an awfully long time since he had enjoyed a good night's sleep. His eyes were red-webbed. The smarting pain in them was beginning to trouble him.

An hour behind Mills, he pulled in at the line shack on Squaw Creek to raid the cache of supplies kept there. He had his breakfast, noting the signs of the man who had stopped here before him, unaware that two other men had stopped here this morning. But after he had eaten and gone out in front of the shack, he saw the fresh tracks of two different horses. One set of tracks, he could be pretty sure, had been left by Mills' horse. About the other, he was puzzled.

He wondered again who besides Mills had been here this morning, then shrugged and turned toward his horse. Before he could swing into the saddle, however, he heard hoofbeats around the shoulder of the hill. He drew his horse into the shelter of the shrubbery lining the creek, and stood there, rigid, his gun in his hand, aware that he wasn't completely hidden.

The man wheeling into view and scanning the area in front of him, was Dan Brewster. He held a rifle in one hand across his saddle and in that first quick look he didn't see Gil's horse. His eyes centered on the line shack. Then he looked down at the ground, probably at the same tracks Gil had noticed. When he looked up again, Gil braced himself. In another moment, in another search of the fringing trees, the man would notice him. Gil could be almost certain of that. He stepped forward, his gun raised. He called, "Here I am, Brewster. Over this way."

Brewster whirled to face him, half lifting his rifle, then lowering it under the threat of the gun which covered him. The look in his eyes was hard, steady, unwavering. For a moment he was silent. Then his words slapped out bitterly.

"Next time, Daly. Next time I'll be the one who has you under a gun."

"If there is a next time," Gil said.

"There will be."

Gil shook his head. "Where were you going?"

"None of your damned business," Brewster snapped.

Gil moved closer to the man. "Two men are ahead of us," he said slowly. "One is Frank Mills. I followed him from Antioch and I had a good idea where he was going. Up the canyon to Pete Enders' camp."

Brewster said nothing.

"I know a little more than I did the last time I talked to you," Gil went on. "I'm pretty sure now that it was Mills who killed Bill Kemp and Pete Enders. I'll know the truth when I get my hands on Mills."

"You'll not get your hands on him down here," Brewster said.

"I know that," Gil agreed.

Dan Brewster wiped the back of one hand across his face. He said, "Colin left the ranch last night to follow Mills to town. I went after him, but Colin didn't go to town. This morning I cut his trail leading this way."

"Then Colin is the other man who stopped here?"

188

Brewster nodded.

"Following Mills, or with him?"

"Following him," Brewster's words were explosive. "No son of mine would ever tie in with a murderer."

"So you agree with me about Frank Mills?"

"But about nothing else. Give me an even break with a gun, Daly."

"No deal, Brewster. I'm too much interested in Frank Mills."

"Then let's get up the canyon and call off our row for a day."

The proposition startled Gil. He stared at Brewster, wondering what driving compulsion was behind it, wondering how seriously Brewster meant it.

"I've never broken a word in my life," Brewster said. "What I'm trying to do is catch up with a headstrong kid. Colin is no match for Mills. You know them both. You know I'm right."

Gil weighed the facts carefully. He could almost believe what Brewster was saying, or at least the part of it about Colin. The relationship he had seen between Colin and Brewster hadn't been close, but after all, Brewster was the young man's father. It wasn't unreasonable that Dan Brewster should be worried.

"How about it, Daly?" Brewster was asking. "Will you take my word?"

"You could shoot me down and no one would ever know you had broken it," Gil said.

"Then take my guns," Brewster roared. "But for God's sake, let's get started."

Gil sighed heavily. He could sense the urgency Brewster was feeling. How far he could trust the man, he didn't know, and he didn't want to find out the hard way. At the same time, he didn't want to feel responsible for having prevented Brewster from helping his son.

"Take my guns," Brewster shouted once more.

He threw his rifle at Gil's feet. He started unbuckling his gun belt.

"Wait a minute," Gil said. "Do I have your word on it? Your word that we forget our row until tomorrow?"

"That's what I said, wasn't it?"

"Say it again."

"Until tomorrow, Gil Daly, I won't lift a gun or a hand against you."

"All right, Brewster. Climb down and pick up your rifle. We'll head up canyon. But you ride first, in front of me."

But even with Dan Brewster riding in front of him, Gil wondered how big a fool a man could be, agreeing to such a deal.

CHAPTER
SIXTEEN

They rode up canyon, Dan Brewster, the owner of Swallowfork, and Gil Daly, the saddle bum from nowhere. They pushed their horses, Gil praying that his would hold up. At first they didn't talk, and Brewster seldom looked back at the man who followed him. But once, when they stopped for a brief rest and Gil had rolled a cigaret, Brewster proffered a match. Another time during a halt, Brewster asked, "What do you think you're going to get out of all this? That is, if you live through it?" And Gil answered, honestly, "A chance to start out again, on my own."

They had one other brief conversation in the late afternoon when they made what would be their last stop. Brewster started it, in a stubborn defense of his own actions.

"I've got only two regrets, Daly. One, I told you about. I should have shot you down when we lynched Farley. The other concerns Myra Chenoweth — but some way I can make that up to her."

"And you have no regrets about Farley?" Gil asked.

Brewster shrugged.

"Or about the death of Howard Logan?"

The older man stiffened. "Logan was a rustler. He'd been stealing Swallowfork cattle for years. He got what he deserved."

"I was with him when he was shot, Brewster. He was fighting for his ranch just as you would fight for yours."

"He was still a rustler."

Gil offered no more argument, sensing the uselessness of it. In Brewster's mind, Logan was a rustler. In all probability, nothing would ever make him think differently.

"And now about Mills," Brewster was saying.

"What about him?"

"Mills is my problem. When we find him, I deal with him."

There was an ugly expression on Brewster's face. A scowl often was there, but now it reflected grim and violent purpose. His hands were tightly clenched. He was leaning toward Gil in an attitude which seemed to demand an immediate agreement.

"Things will work out the way they work out," Gil said coolly. "We haven't found Mills yet."

"Just remember what I said," Brewster growled. "Let's get moving."

They rode on once more, and Gil, looking forward to what they might expect when they reached the old prospector's camp, felt an icy chill race up and down his back. Brewster might want to settle things with Mills, but a settlement could possibly be reached through talk. And if that happened, where would it leave him? A little talk could bring Brewster, Colin and Mills together, with Gil Daly again the outsider.

He checked his gun. He glanced from side to side. The canyon walls were closing in. The creek had become a trickle of water. They were nearing the high plateau where Enders' camp was located.

"We're almost there," he called to Brewster who rode just ahead of him. "The canyon walls come almost together and then widen out again. Pete Enders' camp is against the wall to the left."

Brewster didn't reply. He just drew his rifle from its boot.

They reined up at the edge of the mountain plateau. Here, the high, circling walls of the canyon formed a wide basin, its open areas broken by clumps of trees and shrubbery. In the far end of the basin and around its edges, the forests were more dense. The fresh trails of two horses cut across the clearing, swinging at different angles toward the canyon's high southern wall.

Brewster stared at the ground, studying those trails. After a moment he swung his horse around toward Gil. "Colin went that way," he said, pointing. "They weren't riding together. You can see that yourself."

"Maybe," Gil said.

"We'll stick together," said Brewster. "How close to the camp can we ride without being heard?"

"Well into the trees," Gil answered.

Brewster nodded and started forward. And almost at the same instant Gil heard the high whine of a rifle bullet, followed by the crack of the shot. Brewster lunged in his saddle. Gil thought he had been hit, but when he saw the man driving ahead toward the first fringing trees, he knew he was wrong.

Crouching low over the horn, Gil tore after him. He heard another shot, but it had a different sound this time, a flatter report. And there had been no whine of a bullet. The second shot had come from a six-gun.

This puzzled him. The shots had come from the direction of the old prospector's camp. Why would a man who had a rifle, use a six-gun for his second shot? At the distance they were from the camp, only a rifle could have been effective.

Brewster pulled up at the edge of the trees and looked back, his face showing the strain of anxiety. Assured that Gil was following him, he drove on, taking a twisting course through the trees, still crouched low in the saddle to avoid scraping branches. Twice Gil called to him to bear more to the left. The trees thinned out, then grew more dense, stunted, and tangled with shrubbery. They were climbing now, climbing toward the high wall and the sheltered camp Pete Enders had built, and making as much noise as an army. They were following a foolish and reckless course. Mills or Colin could be hidden in any one of a score of places up ahead. Two well aimed shots would stop pursuit in a hurry.

Gil's gun was in his hand. His eyes jerked from side to side as he followed Brewster's mad course through the trees. It struck him suddenly how easy it would be for Colin and Mills to let Brewster pass and to center both their shots on him, and he started pulling up. But just ahead of him, now, Brewster swung his horse sharply to the right and angled through a thinning fringe of trees toward the clearing.

Gil Daly swerved that way, too. Beyond Brewster's shoulder he saw the crude lean-to shelter Pete Enders had built against the cliff wall, and the tumble of rocks which had once been a cairn over the old prospector's body. He saw nothing else. No sign of Colin or Mills.

Brewster had reined up, and seemed to be listening. Then, as Gil drew near him, a high cry burst from the older man's lips. "Colin! Colin!"

Something had caught Brewster's attention, but what it was, Gil didn't know. He saw Brewster slide to the ground and start running forward, straight toward the camp. He saw him drop to his knees just beyond the mound of rocks which had been rolled from the cairn.

Gil's eyes swept the camp and the fringing trees but he still could detect no signs of Colin or Mills. He swung to the ground, trailed the reins of his horse, and then started forward, half expecting to hear the blast of a shot from somewhere in the trees. But there were no shots, and nearer the camp he saw what Brewster had seen — the crumpled, motionless figure of Colin.

Gil moved closer, circling what was left of the cairn. He stood, finally, almost at Brewster's shoulder. And he could see the spreading stain of blood high on Colin's shirt and could hear Brewster's low voice, calling his son by name, begging him to answer.

But Colin lay as motionless as though dead, his eyes closed, a pallor showing under the tanned skin of his face. He was still breathing. Death hadn't yet reached out and taken him. But death was hovering close. Its promise was in the froth of color bubbling from Colin's lips, and in the slow and labored sound of his breathing.

"Mills did this," Brewster said heavily.

As though in verification of the charge, a rifle bullet snapped in the air close to Gil's ear. He ducked, then dropped swiftly to the ground in the protection of the shelter Pete Enders had built. The echoing blast of the shot came from up the canyon.

Brewster looked around at Gil, his face haggard. Brewster was also flat on the ground.

"I can go after him," Gil said. "You stay with Colin."

"No. We'll both wait here," Brewster said. "Mills won't hang around long."

Colin stirred. Unintelligible sounds came from his lips. Brewster reached out to touch him on the shoulder.

From the edge of the shelter, Gil looked up canyon. Just where Mills was, he couldn't guess, but from the sound of the shot, the man couldn't be far away. And he wouldn't be in a hurry to leave. Gil could be pretty sure of that. The only way Mills could protect the secret of the gold strike was by murdering those who knew it, in the hope that he would finally come to the end of the list. For him and Brewster to stay here and do nothing was suicide.

Gil looked around at Brewster but Brewster was paying no attention to him. He got to his feet and cut toward the trees. The zing of a rifle bullet told him that Mills had spotted him.

"Hey, Daly!" Dan Brewster shouted. "Daly, where do you think you're going?"

196

"After Frank Mills," Gil called back. "I'll bring him here if I can."

He hurried through the trees to where he had left his horse. He swung into the saddle, circled the camp, and pushed on up canyon, keeping close to the canyon wall.

Brewster had drawn his gun, but remembering his promise to Gil Daly, he shoved it back into its holster and listened to the fading sound of Gil's horse, racing up canyon. "I'll never see him again," he muttered. "He'll probably take this chance to get away."

But even as he said that he knew he was wrong about Gil Daly. He had been wrong about the man all along. He had called Daly a saddle bum, and had tried to make that term stick. But the man who had come with him here and who had twice invaded the Swallowfork was a good deal more than a drifting cowhand.

A whisper from Colin drove all thought of Gil Daly from his mind. He moved closer, unbuttoned his son's shirt and examined the ugly wound in his chest.

"There's no use — doing anything about it," Colin said.

Consciousness had returned to him suddenly. His eyes had opened and he was staring at his father. Brewster pulled off his neckerchief. He wiped the froth of blood from Colin's lips.

He said, "Take it easy, Colin. Don't do any talking. You'll pull through all right."

"But I won't," Colin said. "Where's Mills?"

"I'll take care of Mills," Brewster said.

"You should have fired him long ago," Colin said. "It wasn't the ranchers who were taking our cattle. It was Mills and Hondo and Crowell. All of them. They took the cattle in small batches, through the hills, west of Logan's and north of Charlie Weseloh's. A man named Wainwright made the outside arrangements. He comes to Antioch every month or so. He says he's a railroad man but he's really —"

Colin's voice trailed off. He closed his eyes once more. Brewster reached out with his neckerchief and again wiped his son's lips. "Don't try to talk, Colin," he said thickly. "Don't say another word."

Colin's eyes had closed but now he opened them again, and he was frowning. "It was Mills who killed Bill Kemp and Pete Enders," he said slowly, his voice much weaker. "He knew about the gold. He said I should run Swallowfork and he would work here until we had cleaned up. When you rode into sight he lifted his rifle and aimed it at you and said he would do what I didn't have the nerve to do. That's when I jumped him. That's when —"

An expression of pain crossed the young man's face. A shudder ran over his body. His eyes closed once more.

Brewster smoothed his hand over his son's forehead. There were tears on his cheeks. His eyes were bright, his habitual scowl was gone. "You did that for me, Colin?" he whispered. "You did it for me?"

There was an almost reverent note in Brewster's voice. Whatever Colin had done that was wrong, he could forget or forgive in the light of this final act of

198

devotion. Here was something which touched the core of his loneliness. It was something he would cling to, something he would have to remember in the long and empty days ahead.

He fumbled for Colin's hand, and knelt there, holding it, feeling closer to his son than he had for a long time. Feeling as close as he had felt years ago when Colin had been a little boy, and when his mother had been alive, and when life on the Swallowfork had been good.

From up the canyon he heard a burst of gunfire, the sharp crack of a rifle, the flatter sound of a six-gun, each fired several times. But he hardly lifted his head. He had only a vague, detached interest in what was happening up canyon. He was watching Colin's face, waiting for Colin's eyes to open once more, even though he knew that Colin had slipped away from him forever.

CHAPTER
SEVENTEEN

Up the canyon, Gil Daly crouched close to the ground and in the shelter of an outcropping boulder near the canyon wall. Two of the rifle shots Brewster had heard had chipped the boulder inches from his head. His answering fire had driven Mills to a similar protection, higher up on a ledge climbing the wall, which at this point leaned away from the basin. A few moments earlier, in another, exchange of shots, Gil had brought down Mills' horse, blocking any chance the man had for a quick escape.

Mills could still get away, of course. Gil's horse was tied back in the trees. If Mills could reach it, he could have it. The situation boiled down to as simple a fact as that. Between them, he and Mills owned the horse. Whichever one of them lived to reach it, could claim it and ride off.

Gil took a quick look around the edge of the boulder. He saw Mills scrambing up the ledge made by a sloping shelf of rock. The man was a good thirty or forty yards from where he had been a moment before, and was moving fast, awfully fast considering the chunky build of his body. Gil's arm swept up and he fired. Mills immediately swung back of the protection of the rough wall of the cliff. Gil drove another bullet at the point where the man had disappeared, then came to his feet, circled the boulder and raced after him. He covered half the distance before he took shelter again, this time right up against the cliff wall, and on the same narrow ledge as Mills.

Where the ledge would lead them, Gil didn't know. It might climb all the way to the top, but there seemed to be a break ahead, or a bend in the wall. Which it was, he couldn't tell. And perhaps that wasn't important. Mills wasn't trying to get away. There would be no escape for him on foot, and he knew it. In hurrying up this ledge he might have been looking for a place where he could cut back and get above and behind the man who was following him. Or he may have been seeking some other vantage point, where he could lie in wait. For this was a duel from which only one would escape.

Gil stood close against the cliff wall, breathing heavily. After a moment he leaned forward and took a quick look up the ledge. He saw no sign of Mills, but that didn't mean anything. Mills hadn't shot at him, but that didn't mean anything, either. Mills might have found the place he wanted and might have settled down to wait for one good, clean finishing shot.

The sun had dropped from sight only a moment ago, but already the shadows in the valley below were thickening. In another hour it would be growing dark. In another hour, a man couldn't be sure of his footing on this ledge. Gil edged forward, staying close to the cliff wall, moving hurriedly from one jutting protection to another.

Above him he heard a rattling sound. Several small stones, loosened from somewhere higher on the cliff, bounced past him and through the clatter they made he heard a deeper, rumbling roar which seemed to shake the face of the cliff. He knew, instantly, what had happened, and a sharp and almost blinding fear struck him. Mills hadn't stopped and waited at the point where he'd ducked from sight. He had climbed on to the top of the cliff, then turned back. He had started rolling rocks from the top. He had loosened the shell of the cliff somewhere above and the resulting avalanche would sweep everything in front of it.

Gil broke away from his shelter. He started running up the ledge. A cascade of small rocks struck his shoulder, pulling at him, trying to carry him away. He dived forward, clawing for a hold. He got to his knees and clawed on. He felt the ledge dropping away. He rolled with it, still fighting in the loose rock for something firm, something he could grip and hang on to. And he found it, his knee braced between rocks, his fingers clutching the lower rim of a crevice.

The roar of the avalanche lifted all around him and a fine, silt-like dust seemed to bloom up from the base of the cliff. Gil started climbing. In a moment he lay flat and breathless on the edge of a shelf of rock which the avalanche hadn't touched. Behind him, the rest of the shelf was gone, swept away. The fringe of the avalanche had touched him, had caught him up for a moment, and then had let him go.

He stood up, leaning back against the cliff, breathing deeply. His body was covered with perspiration. His fingers were cut, bleeding. He had lost his gun. But he was still alive, and perhaps Mills didn't know that. His quick run up the ledge had given him another chance. That is, if he moved quickly. If he could get to Mills before Mills knew he had escaped.

Just a little distance ahead Gil saw a break in the face of the cliff. Mills might have made his way to the top through this jagged draw. He started that way himself, fighting up through the tangled rocks and underbrush which seemed to be trying to hold him back. He pulled into the clear on the top of the cliff and he saw Mills not a dozen yards away. The chunky, thick-bodied man was at the very edge, leaning forward, staring down. Mills' holster was empty. His rifle stood against a rock near him, a rock similar to the one he must have rolled over the edge to start the avalanche.

Gil lunged, scrambled toward the rifle. Mills heard him. Gil had known he would. But Mills would have heard him even if he had tried to crawl cautiously, and then he would have had no chance at the rifle at all. This way he did have a chance. This way, Mills jerked around and saw him plunging forward, and for an instant the shock of realizing he had escaped held the man motionless.

That instant was enough. Mills grabbed for the rifle and whipped it up, but too late. Gil's hand caught the lifting barrel and thrust it aside, Mills swinging with it. They came together, then, struggling over the rifle. Mills went down, with Gil on top. They rolled over, away from the cliff.

203

It was like that at first, each struggling for the rifle, each with one hand on it, each striking at the other, slugging, jabbing, slugging again. They had come to grips at last, Gil and the man he had been seeking since his first trip up this canyon, the man responsible for all that had happened.

Here they would end it, one way or the other. That knowledge was in each of them. It burned in the black, squinting eyes of Frank Mills. It was reflected in the tight, strained expression on Gil's face.

The chunky man was hard to hold. His body was a round bundle of muscles. He released the rifle when Gil got his knee on it. His hands fastened on Gil's throat. It took a blow in the groin to break that hold, but Gil broke it and then stood up. He didn't have to haul Mills to his feet for Mills was up just as quickly. Mills was bulling in at him, screaming profanity at the top of his lungs, promising what he would do.

Gil met the rush, standing his ground, slugging back, matching blow for blow. He shouted at Mills without knowing it, charging the man with the murder of Pete Enders, the shooting of Bill Kemp, the slaying of Howard Logan, mocking him with the promise of failure. He staggered Mills with a solid blow to the jaw. He followed this up with another. He plowed in and felt the jarring smash of Mills' fists. They ripped at his face, stopping him, driving him back. He tripped, went down, got up again. And he knew that this couldn't go on. He had been weary before the day started. He had taken a beating from the avalanche. How much more could he stand?

204

Mills was driving in at him. He met the man once more, taking all Mills could throw at him, giving back all he could. He ripped another blow at Mills' face, and another, and he saw the chunky man stagger. He surged forward, swinging madly, and at last he saw Mills go down.

Mills was slower getting up this time. When he did get up he held a jagged rock in each hand. His face was contorted. There was an insane look in his eyes. An arm whipped back and then forward, hurling one of the rocks at Gil's head. Gil ducked. Another rock came at him. He ducked again, and out of the corner of his eye, saw that he had backed almost over the edge of the cliff.

He stepped forward but Mills was charging at him now, diving at him. There wasn't a chance to dance away. He felt the thudding blow of the chunky body hitting him, and he twisted as he fell, twisted sideways, clawing for a hold in the earth, jerking his knees up into Mills' face, straightening his legs again. He heard a scream from Mills a high, piercing scream weighted with terror. There was a heavy, dragging weight on his legs, pulling them out over the edge of the cliff. It was there, and then it was gone, and he was alone on the cliff top. Alone and flat on the ground, his fingers bleeding in a crack of rock, his body half over the edge. And echoing in his ears was a last, wavering cry from Frank Mills.

After a time he pulled himself away from the edge. Later, he looked down. He thought he could see a crumpled, motionless figure lying among the rocks at the foot of the cliff. But it was getting dark down there. He couldn't be sure. He must make sure, however. He wouldn't be able to rest until he did.

He started climbing back down into the basin. He would have another cairn of rocks to build, now — a cairn higher than the one he had piled up over the body of Old Pete Enders. Frank Mills had earned a really imposing marker for his grave . . .

The sun had come up and gone down again before Gil Daly reached Antioch. He halted at the outskirts of town, uncertain of what reception he might expect or what the sheriff's attitude might be. He was gaunt, haggard. He hadn't shaved. He was too tired to think very clearly. But after a moment's delay he rode on, and deeper in the town he heard someone call his name, call it out sharply. He pulled up once more, startled.

He heard his name again. "Gil! Gil Daly!" And from the shadow-veiled porch of one of the houses along the street, a figure moved out toward him, running. A tall, slender, boyish figure which he recognized instantly. He swung to the ground as Myra came up, and afterwards he was never to know whether Myra came racing all the way into his arms, or whether he had dismounted and rushed to clasp her tightly to his chest. But regardless, it was good. And his kiss, this time, was neither clumsy nor hurried. It was solid and real and had meaning.

After a while he drew back, stared down at the girl's face, into the warm depths of her eyes. He murmured her name for no other reason than to hear it.

"That's Jean's house where I was waiting," Myra whispered. "I've been watching the road for you all day.

I would have waited all night. I knew you would be coming. Did you — is Mills —"

"Mills will never trouble us again," Gil said bleakly.

He could feel Myra shudder. Then he heard her saying, "Dan Brewster came in to town about an hour ago. He told about how he had met you and the way Colin died. He told us what Colin said before he died, about how Mills and the others had been responsible for the rustling. He's offered to make good any charges leveled against him. He's a broken man, Gil. It's almost as though he had died with Colin."

"Part of him did," said Gil. "But there's iron in Dan Brewster. He'll find a reason to live again."

"The sheriff wants to see you, of course. He was going to lead a posse out tomorrow after Mills. Last night, at the Swallowfork, they got part of the story from Mills' wife. But they didn't know where Mills or Colin or Brewster had gone."

Gil straightened. He said, "Myra, when I go in to see the sheriff, I'd sort of like to be a man with a job. If that job you offered me on your place is still open —"

"You know it is," Myra said quickly. "But I've got to tell you this. The sheriff found Pete Enders' record book in his pocket when he searched the body several days ago. The secret of the gold strike is in that book. Men will soon be heading up the canyon to stake their claims. If you want to go —"

Gil Daly shook his head. "I'm a cattleman, not a prospector, Myra. I've thought it all out. I'll earn whatever comes to me through work I know."

"Then that's settled," Myra said, and her happiness rang true in her voice. It was in the confident glow of her face, and in the tight pressure of her fingers on his arms.

Gil's smile came back. He had nothing to worry about, now. Nothing that he wasn't equal to. He wasn't a man alone any more, a saddle bum drifting through the country. He moved on down the street with Myra, his arm around her waist, her arm around him. This was the way it would be in the years ahead — the two of them together, facing whatever the future might hold.